THE SEARCH

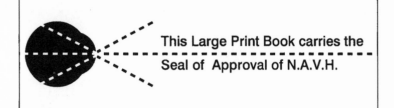

This Large Print Book carries the
Seal of Approval of N.A.V.H.

A BEN SYLVESTER MYSTERY
BOOK 1

THE SEARCH

William Badke

Thorndike Press • Thorndike, Maine

Copyright © 1995 by William Badke

This book is a work of fiction, and all the characters in this novel are fictional. Any resemblance to actual persons, living or dead, is purely coincidental. All of the locations, except for Electar, are real. The dog "Killer" is based on a real animal of the same name and description.

Published in 1999 by arrangement with
Multnomah Publishers, Inc.

Thorndike Large Print ® Christian Mystery Series.

The tree indicium is a trademark of Thorndike Press.

The text of this Large Print edition is unabridged.
Other aspects of the book may vary from the original edition.

Set in 16 pt. Plantin by Minnie B. Raven.

Printed in the United States on permanent paper.

Library of Congress Cataloging in Publication Data

Badke, William B., 1949–
    The search / William Badke.
        p. (large print) cm.
    ISBN 0-7862-1967-X (lg. print : hc : alk. paper)
    1. Large type books. I. Title.
    [PS3552.A318S4   1999]
    813'.54—dc21   99-21868

To my friend and colleague
Herb Sturhahn,
who shares my interest in good stories and
dynamic Christian faith.

My thanks to my editor, Rod Morris, for his keen perception and ready encouragement.

ONE

I dodged him, surprising myself, and the knife missed my heart. But I felt it slice deep into my upper left arm — no pain yet, just the sick knowledge that my body had been invaded. I was in trouble. The knife swung again. He was over-extended, and it went past me.

So I ran. I bolted down the hill, through the ferns and vines, tripping and sliding, with the big man behind me, moving fast. Once he fell hard, the air going out of him like a burst tire, and almost as noisy. But he was too tough to be stopped that way, by accident, and I heard him crashing behind me again.

Every part of me ached with the whipping of shrubs and the forcing of muscles far beyond any of the feeble training I had given them lately. I ran when I could, crawled when I had to, not knowing my direction anymore, my lungs shrieking at me to give it up. The big man, booze and a probable lifetime of cigarettes getting to him, began to fade.

Then I was through. A road. Cars. Lots of them. I flagged a taxi, empty for a change, and slumped into the back seat, trying to hide the wound and at the same time keep it away from the filthy vinyl I was sitting on. The driver was barely paying attention to the road, let alone me. At his rate of speed — impossibly fast, like all the rest of the traffic — we'd be at the embassy in ten minutes. Now I was getting thirsty. A bad sign. I'd lost a lot of blood. My mind was starting to drift too. Stay awake.

I wasn't trained for this. Other people did the rough stuff. I was supposed to be an analyst, an advisor. Stay awake. Angry that they put me in a position like that. We were supposed to have people on the ground to keep the lunatic fringe away from the analysts. Nobody even gave me any cover that I could see.

They just let me walk into it like a lamb to —

"Mister, you okay?" The driver sounded so far away I could scarcely connect with him.

"Okay," I said, lifting up my head. "Embassy."

"I get you there. No sweat."

Most of the rest was a fog. We stopped. A guard's face. They were carrying me. When

I woke up, I was in some bedroom, the ceiling fan above me rumbling slightly with every turn. No pictures on the walls.

I remembered my arm and twisted my head to look at it. Bandaged. It looked professional, the gauze tied flat and no blood showing. There wasn't much pain. They must have given me something for the pain. I drifted off.

When I woke again, they were waiting, two men in suits, looking official. Neither of them seemed very happy. But then I wasn't ecstatic myself. "Go away," I muttered, not sure my whisper was loud enough to be heard, not caring either. The ceiling fan cast a shadow over me that danced on and off like a slow strobe light.

"We figured you'd be the nasty type considering your line of work," one of them said, his voice coming down a long tunnel, echoing off the walls so that it sounded as if his mouth was lined with tin. I stared at him, not really seeing him but trying to win the advantage. There was no way I wanted to talk to these guys.

They waited, knowing that I wasn't in any shape to be belligerent for long. I thought about it, the very process of thinking taking more out of me than I had to give. Clearly, I had no resources to lie there in silence while they badgered me. "Okay," I said, weary. "You ask the questions. I'll tell the lies."

"We're from the embassy." It didn't seem to matter which one of them spoke. They were the same person in two bodies.

"You're not traveling salesmen? I need some new items for my widget collection." It took considerable effort, but the effect was worth it.

"Look, Mr. Sylvester, it wasn't us who brought you here. You made that choice yourself."

"I needed protection."

"You've got a serious knife wound." I wasn't paying attention to which one of them was talking. It didn't matter. "So tell us about it."

"A bad man wanted my wallet. I said no."

"Come on. We're not idiots."

"You're not?" For a second I thought he was going to pound me into the mattress.

One of them walked away across the room and then turned to face me, as if he'd rehearsed it. "Your name is Benjamin Sylvester. You work for Libertec, a company that specializes in counseling emerging nations on the ins and outs of democratic government. You were here to do exactly what?"

This last was spoken in the same monotone as the rest, and it took me a few seconds to realize he had asked a question.

"Vacation," I muttered. "Sand and surf."

"So why weren't you at the beach today?"

"Sunburn." Both of them sneered.

"Did anyone ever tell you you're obnoxious?"

"My wife, the kids, my boss, the paper-boy —"

"Give us a break. What are we supposed to tell the ambassador?" They looked at each other, but it was clear that neither of them knew how to proceed if torture was denied to them.

"I don't have to talk to you. Tell him I'm psychologically incompetent since the incident. Get him to ship me home."

"Look, Sylvester, you wandered in here covered with blood. We gave you a doctor and a bed."

"So send me a bill. And put a nice tip on it for yourselves."

They left before I managed to ask them if I could make a long distance phone call. They probably would have bugged it anyway. Sure I was hostile. The company I work for is not exactly bold about publicity. We operate in the background, for reasons I find obvious even if other people think I should risk my hide every time I take on a job.

11

I know I was taking it out on the wrong people, but I was furious that my company had messed it up and landed me in the middle of an interrogation. They were supposed to protect me. Valuable property and all that. Some clumsy oaf somewhere had miscalculated. It was supposed to be a simple entry and exit — meet with a small group of intellectuals, convince them that I knew my subject, and establish a communication system so we could work with them. These guys had stayed so secret there was no reason for anyone to believe they even knew each other.

The two clowns from the embassy were at least right about Libertec. We're a private consulting firm that helps democracies to emerge and emerging democracies to get better at it. But I have a degree in political science, for crying out loud, not Kung Fu or footboxing. Someone should have protected me.

Once I showed them that I knew my rights, everything moved fast. By the next morning I was on a plane for Seattle. It was made obvious to me that they'd bill me for the flight, and the doctor, and the accommodation — maybe even a tip for the two clowns I'd talked to. And I still hadn't made my phone call.

Seattle was wet, with an early November chill that promised a winter of watching my knuckles for signs of early arthritis. I hate that nasty bite on my face, raindrops attacking my skin like hungry insects. The traffic was bad too, once I'd collected my car and headed north for Bellingham.

I only stopped once — at a phone booth at a rest area to call Libertec and unload some of my anger. Simpson, the VP of operations, pleaded innocent. This was supposed to have been a low-risk operation. I was playing tourist in a tourist country, and my contact was a taxi driver —

"— who took me into the jungle and then tried to knife me when I got out of the car."

"Did you see anyone else?"

"No."

"So why'd you get out of the cab?"

"He said we'd arrived. My contacts were supposedly waiting in a clearing just a little way down a path."

"So did your assailant" — I loved Simpson's appreciation for official terminology — "did your assailant give you any reasons for his attack?"

"No. I guess he realized that I knew he didn't like me, and so he wanted to end the relationship." Confusing talk usually baffles Simpson.

"Go home," he said. "Take a week. We'll work on it."

"You'd better." I hung up.

Later, driving, the rain coming down harder, I started to wonder again why I'd ever joined that dizzy company with all its bizarre missions to save the world from tyranny, other than the fact that the money was good. I'm as much a believer in democracy as the next guy, but I expect at least a little gratitude from our clients, not a knife in the arm.

Karen didn't deserve that kind of life either — me gone most of the time, with her father phoning her once a week, begging her to dump me and take over his company before he cashed in his chips. But dwelling on Jim Barker did nothing for my anger, so I dropped it. Too much adrenaline already. It made my arm hurt more than ever.

Dusk was falling when I pulled off I-5 and skirted the edge of Bellingham, heading north on the Guide-Meridian toward Lynden. Strange people there — lots of transplanted Hollanders and churchgoers. You could barely buy a chocolate bar there on Sunday morning. But they kept their houses painted and their lawns cut. A person could eat a wet salad off a sidewalk and not have to chew on a single grain of sand.

Karen chose it. She hated Seattle. So what if it meant an incredible commute for me if the town made her feel secure. Karen valued security. Understandable with a past like hers. Maybe that was why she had gotten so much into religion in the last few months.

Karen's religion was starting to worry me. I knew she was happier, but she had the kids down at the church Sundays and Tuesday nights and even a few Saturday mornings. It would only be a matter of time before my little guys started grousing, and then I'd be caught in the middle. Lately she'd been trying to let me know that she was moving toward some major decisions about her faith.

I loved her, but she had always been elusive, hard to reach. Her past lurked in her eyes, a barrier to her soul, as if part of her was somewhere else, locked in a hidden room deep inside. I admit that I was attracted by the mystery, the intrigue of trying to discover who she was, or who she would have been, given another father. But it was frustrating because she could so easily hide herself when she was hurting, when I could have helped her.

I moved the car quickly along the straight road, soggy farmland on both sides, dairy cows being herded home to earn their keep in the milking barns. The rain was letting up, and the radio forecast promised clouds but little precipitation for the next week. It wasn't hard to admit that Karen had been right about the peace here, as if another era had been transplanted and we had been given the privilege of living in it so that we could escape the hostility of the urban now.

I pulled over at a Chevron station at the Pole Road intersection and used a phone booth to call Karen. She wasn't expecting me for a few more days, and I knew she hated surprises. But there wasn't any answer, even though I let it ring fifteen times or so. Strange. It was close to five, and she always made sure she was there before the kids got home from school.

My stomach tightened just a bit and my shoulder started to throb again. It was only six or seven minutes to the house, a wood frame bungalow we'd gotten for a song. One of these days I was going to add a few rooms but —

The house was dark, and I was sure something was wrong. She might be at a neighbor's house, but she was too concerned about security to leave the house alone after dark unless I was with her. I hit the brakes and bolted for the front door.

It wasn't locked. I scrambled for the light

switch. There was nothing there. I mean nothing — no sofa, no chairs, no sideboard, no dining room table. Bare from wall-to-wall. Dazed, not understanding, I wandered through. The whole place was as empty as if it had just been built. Not a stick of furniture, nothing but the carpet.

In our bedroom, I spotted a piece of paper on the floor, picked it up, and unfolded it. The words made no sense to me:

Ben,
I'm leaving you. That's something you might not recognize right away, because you're never here anyway, and you hardly notice us when you are. Don't try to find us. You can keep the cat. None of us wants him.

She didn't sign it, didn't need to. Slowly the numbness passed so I could read it again. Especially the last two sentences, and the panic hit me so hard I almost fell. This was all wrong, the house, Karen, the kids. They were in danger, and my first temptation was to bolt for the police, the army, whatever.

"You can keep the cat. None of us wants him." We didn't own a cat. Never had.

I didn't hear him come in. Probably I'd

left the front door open. Probably he had a key anyway. From the corner of my eye I saw movement, and I turned to stare head on into the biggest pistol barrel I had ever seen.

TWO

There is something about a gun six inches from your left eye that moves you down to the primordial instincts of breathing and survival. It hypnotized me, capturing my mind, so that there was nothing in the world but a pistol, a hand, and me.

"Step back." The voice was low and harsh. With difficulty I connected the sound to the man's form behind the gun. I stepped back. "Sit on the floor. Back against the wall. Legs stretched out." I obeyed.

"Where's my wife and kids?"

"They went away. You've got the note in your hand."

"She wrote it, but I don't believe it. Did you kidnap them?"

"No. Did the note say anything about a cat?"

"Yes."

"Too bad." I studied him. Fortyish. Curly brown hair, graying slightly. Square jaw. Looked tough. Dressed in jeans and a black canvas jacket. Running shoes.

"Why?" I asked.

"The note was only partly for your benefit. It was mainly for me."

"Where are my wife and kids?"

"I haven't got them. Honest."

"Then why the gun?"

"Because we have to go somewhere, and I didn't think you'd come willingly."

"What if I won't go?"

"I know what happened to your wife."

"You said you didn't have her."

"I don't. But I know what happened."

"So tell me."

"Can't do that."

"What about the kids?"

"They're probably safe. Don't worry about them."

I was coming unglued. Too much was happening too fast. "Is Karen in danger?"

"I don't think so. Not for now, anyway."

"Let me put this slowly: What . . . is . . . going . . . *on?*"

For a second he looked genuinely grieved. "I can't tell you," he said. "It wouldn't be good for you to know. Could you trust me that things will probably work themselves out?"

"No! I want my wife and kids back!" The screaming I heard was me, fury detaching my rational mind from the animal underneath. I called him everything I could think of, the fear demolished by rage. He just stood there blinking.

After a few seconds of silence, he murmured, "Are you done?"

"I won't be done until I get them back!"

"We have to get going."

"Where?"

"Across the border."

"You're not getting me to hop ditches. A person could get shot."

"No, we're driving across at the Aldergrove checkpoint."

"And I'm just supposed to go with you, meek as a lamb?"

"Don't forget that I know what happened to your wife. You turn me in and you're on your own."

"This is insane." I flung my head back against the wall, hard. It didn't help much. Think. Calm down. Try to understand it.

But nothing made sense. Karen didn't walk out on people. It wasn't her way. She would have stayed to explain if there really was a problem. And the bit about the cat had to be a signal. Who would kidnap her and the kids? Why take all the furniture? Now to top it off, I had this maniac with a gun in my face.

"What's happening?" I said, crumbling, my voice shaking with frustration.

"Are you ready to go?" He didn't seem to have heard my question.

"No."

"Look, Ben, you're going to have to trust me —"

"— said the kidnapper as he held a gun to my head."

"I don't intend to hurt you."

"So put the pistol away."

"You won't go with me if I do."

"Will you shoot me if I don't?"

"You're not thinking clearly. I know what happened to Karen. You have no choice. But if you want an answer, I might have to deal you a flesh wound or something. I'll do whatever it takes to get you to Canada." He didn't seem to believe his own words. Was he softening?

"I've already got a flesh wound."

"How did that happen?" he asked, as if he had only just then noticed my sling.

"Knife in the arm. My employers think it goes with the territory."

The guy stepped back. "Stand up. We have to get going."

"Tell me why."

"Just move it!" I could hear the tension in his voice. "You're in danger here." As soon as he said it, I knew he'd made some kind of tactical error. I bore in.

"Danger? From who?"

"I can't tell you." The guy was shriveling in front of me. The bravado was fading so fast I would have given him only a few seconds to break into tears. Then, strangely, he got ahold of himself. "We're going now." The way he put it, I started to believe he might plug me in the other arm to convince me he was serious.

"All right." I got up. What was I supposed to do anyway? "Whose car?"

"Yours. You drive."

"It's hard going with this sling. And what am I supposed to tell them at the border?"

"There's a Benedictine monastery in Mission, across the Fraser River. Tell them we're going to a retreat there for a week."

"Are we?"

"No." The look on his face might have been guilt.

"Will they believe me?"

"I hope so."

"What if I scream blue murder instead?"

"Then they'll arrest me, and you might never see your family again. Look, man . . ." He leveled the gun at me. "We're not playing some stupid game here, you and I." He'd probably borrowed the line from an old movie, but it was convincing.

We walked outside. My suitcase was in the

trunk. His was on the porch, and he picked it up on the way to the car. The gun wasn't very important anymore, because he knew he'd won me over. I had no choice but to go with him.

He made me drive, clumsy with the sling. We left Lynden, picked up the Guide-Meridian, and headed to the border, bumping along the rough, narrow pavement that led to Canada. "What do I call you?" I muttered.

"Bob's okay."

"Not your real name."

"No."

"Fine, Bob. Does this power trip make you feel good?"

"No."

"You wish you were doing something else tonight?"

He didn't answer, and there was not much time for further conversation during the five-mile trip. We slowed down once so he could throw the gun in a creek. Traffic was light, and then we were there, the red building bold in my headlights.

"American citizens?"

"Yes."

"What's the purpose of your visit?"

"We're going to a retreat at the monastery in Mission."

"What retreat?"

I panicked but Bob chipped in: "We teach at a Bible college. There's a reading break on, so we booked into the Abbey for a few days. The rest of us are crossing at Sumas."

The customs man stared at us for a few seconds. I forced myself to look him in the eye. We tried to read each other like a game of cat and mouse without the movement. Then he said, "Enjoy yourselves," and we were through.

The road widened immediately and got smoother, as if the Canadians made a bigger deal of going stateside than we did traveling to Canada.

At first I didn't recognize the sound, and then I realized that Bob was singing to himself, very softly with a fast, jerky rhythm, the tune unrecognizable. His fingers were drumming on the dashboard, but it wasn't joy. His face showed pure anguish.

A few miles further north, we spotted a McDonald's and Bob suggested we stop for coffee.

"You're the tour guide," I said wearily.

"So welcome to Aldergrove."

"I've been here before."

"Well, you're here again."

He giggled. I looked at him sharply. Crossing the border had broken down his tough facade, and I could see his fear, naked and unchecked. This guy, who was just holding on by the skin of his teeth, was my only link to Karen and the kids. If he snapped, I'd be left with nothing.

"Fine. Coffee."

He made me drive around to the front of the restaurant, and we parked under a light. As he got out, he turned in a slow half circle and then smiled.

"Something strike you funny, Bob?"

"Yeah. Let's get our coffee."

The place was three-quarters full, something which seemed to please Bob even more. We sat near the back, around the corner from the front windows.

"You don't like me very much, do you, Ben?"

"Sure I do. You may have turned me into your loyal slave, but you bought me coffee. I think you're terrific."

"You're kind of big on sarcasm."

"Do tell."

"Look, Ben, you're going to have to co-operate. Just out there, parked beside your car, are two guys who followed us from Lynden." I gaped at him. "We're leaving by the back door. You go into the washroom, wait thirty seconds, then move out through that door" — he indicated with his eyes —

"nice and easy. Try to use people as shields between you and the front windows. There's a blue Honda Civic right outside. Canadian plates."

"What about my car?"

"Sorry. They'll probably impound it."

"Thanks a lot. And then they'll organize a search party for me."

"But you'll have vanished."

"What about this?" I pointed at my sling.

"I don't get you."

"It makes me conspicuous. Someone's bound to remember me and the fact that I was in here with you."

"So? We're not going to be using my car or yours. I borrowed the Civic. And the plates are just muddy enough to make them un-readable. The rain, you know. Come on, Ben. You don't want to meet those guys out there, believe me."

"Okay." I was too overwhelmed to fight him. Two minutes later, we were both in the car and headed out the back driveway, Bob at the wheel. We didn't turn on the lights until we reached the main street. No one seemed to be following us.

We wound through back roads for several miles, the rain over but the pavement wet and hissing under our tires. It all seemed to be farmland, what I could see of it. Once we crossed under a freeway. The countryside was more rolling than Lynden, but it seemed to be the same sort of economy.

"Where are we going?" I asked finally, condemning myself for revealing weakness. I should have waited so that he wouldn't know how troubled I was.

"Other side of Mission. Northeast." He was getting cryptic, clipping his words as he concentrated on the road.

"This doesn't make any sense."

"Not supposed to."

"Are you working for the people who took my wife and kids?" I almost caught him on that one. He should have answered "yes" or "no," and then I would have known it had been a kidnapping.

"Nobody took your family. They left."

"Then why am I here?"

"Can't tell you."

"Do you know?"

"Yes."

I was seething, but it did no good. Instead, I clammed up and watched what little I could see of the scenery in the dark. After about twenty minutes we came to a highway, then a long bridge across the Fraser River.

"Mission," Bob said, as the lights of the small city glittered at us.

"We told the border guard we were coming here. Not very smart."

"Sure it was. We're not going to the monastery. If anyone checks, they'll think the whole story was a red herring. The last thing they'll suspect is that we'll be only about ten miles from there."

We turned east on the Lougheed Highway, past a lake on the left, and then north at a Shell station. "Where does this go?" I asked him.

"About ten miles north. Then it's all logging roads deep into the mountains. Beautiful spot." He giggled again. "Did you notice the name of the road we're on? Sylvester Road. One of your relatives, Ben?"

"Who cares? What's the point of small talk when I'm out one family and some maniac is taking me into the deep woods of Canada." How much else did he know about me? He had my name down pat even though it wasn't on our mailbox.

"I resent your use of the term *maniac*."

"If the shoe fits . . ."

The road began to wind. Even in the darkness I could see that we were ringed by mountains a thousand feet high. A far cry from the plains twenty miles south.

"How much farther?"

"A few miles."

We crossed a bridge, and in the headlights I saw a wide rocky creek. Then, about a mile later, Bob suddenly turned sharply and appeared to be about to drive right up the hill face. We bounced up a narrow road, steep and rough, then swung left at the top and stopped on the level. The lights shone on a small house, totally dark.

Immediately, the air was full of the roaring bark of a large, black dog — a lab or a shepherd — chained to the side of the house. "Watch out for the dog," Bob said. "He means it."

"Is the chain strong enough?"

"Probably. If it breaks, go down on your knees and beg for mercy. It might help to weep a bit."

"What's that beast's name?"

"Killer," he said, and there was no trace of humor in his voice.

THREE

I awoke disoriented, staring at rough walls in the semi-darkness. It was cold, and my arm ached. Gradually the memories of the past night became focused, pushing away the fog. I reached up and turned on the light.

At least Bob had given me my own room, even if it was a bit rustic. No drapes on the window, no need of any. I looked outside, where I could discern the vague ominous shape of a giant mountain right in front of the house, across a narrow valley.

My watch read half past seven. With the mountain in front, the sun wouldn't be up for some time. The sound of pots rattling led me to the kitchen. Bob was frying bacon and eggs — a picture of domestic bliss. I felt another twinge of fury at the stupidity of my situation, but I suppressed it. Cold reason was the only thing that was going to convince this guy to open up to me. Or maybe torture.

"Morning." He smiled.

"Save it. I hope you can cook."

"I'm a bachelor and I'm still healthy. Sure I can cook."

"Do you live here?"

"Are you kidding? It's borrowed. Even the dog's borrowed."

"Why?"

"Let's eat," he said. "I hope the coffee's not too strong." Bob seemed to major in evasion. It was almost impossible for me to make sense of him. Somehow he was all wrong for this job, despite his outward toughness.

As we ate, I started to work on the edges. "Some kid's going to find that pistol you threw in the creek before we crossed the border."

"So?" he said. "It was a replica. A nice toy, nothing more."

"You held me up with a toy gun?"

"Nobody gets hurt that way." I could see the anxiety starting to build in him again.

"You're not cut out for this."

"Probably not. But I'm in it now. Don't expect to find me backing down."

"Why the borrowed dog?"

"Everyone's got a dog around here. Bears, cougars, bobcats — who knows what you might face when you step out the door?"

"How about the two goons who followed us from Lynden? Is the dog for them?"

"They're long gone."

"I doubt it."

"Dogs are good for all kinds of things," he said, munching his bacon.

I ate fast, then went outside. Bob didn't try to stop me. Squatting just beyond the range of the dog's chain, I said quietly, "Morning, Killer." He sprang against the chain so fast and hard I almost fell over backwards. Luckily, the bolt that attached his tether to the side of the house was at least half an inch thick. He roared that typical shepherd bark — woof, woof, woof, woof, woof — the last one at a lower pitch, as if he'd finished that round and was getting ready for the next. Killer was not going to make friends easily. A magnificent beast really, pure black, muscles everywhere, teeth pointed and glistening. But I wasn't paying attention to the dog anymore. It was time to make plans.

Bob had made me his unshackled prisoner because of what he knew, and it was time to turn the tables. Once he told me his secrets, I wouldn't need him. Old Bob would be left behind like yesterday's news, and I would gain control. This, of course, meant I'd have to get rough. I wasn't planning to hurt him badly, but my stomach tensed at the thought of what I might have to do to make him talk. The key was to catch him off guard. And I had to do it soon.

It turned out to be far easier than I thought it would be. I spotted a piece of two-by-four about three feet long. It was inside Killer's range, but I didn't have much trouble deking out the dog with fancy footwork and grabbing the board. I pulled off my sling, wincing at the ache in my arm. I positioned myself around the corner of the house and shouted, "Bob, hurry! There's something wrong with Killer!"

Sure enough, he came trotting around the corner, and I whacked him full across the stomach with the two-by-four. He went down like he'd been shot, gasping for air, retching. I felt sick.

I dragged him inside and tied him to a chair with some twine I found on a shelf. He was in no shape to resist me. In fact, he didn't seem too aware of his surroundings. I took a quick look at the bandage on my arm. No blood, only pain. The stitches had held.

"Bob." I grabbed his jaw and positioned his head so that he had to look me in the face. "Bob, do you know what's happening?"

He grunted and tried to pull away. I hung on. "You need to tell me some things. If you don't, I'm going to hurt you even worse." He stared at me for a few seconds, his mind clearing and then — I couldn't believe it —

34

he started to laugh, low like a whisper of mirth, as if it would hurt him to make it any more boisterous. It probably would.

"Are you okay?" I heard myself asking foolishly.

He had trouble saying it, but he got it out: "Open my shirt."

"What?"

"I said open my shirt."

"Why?"

"To see how" — he paused for breath — "idiotic this is."

"I'd rather not."

"Humor me."

"Why?"

"Because you're wasting your time trying to beat the truth out of me."

Reluctantly, I undid a few buttons, and he saw me wince before I could avoid it. His chest was covered with dozens of small scars, the size a cigarette would make. I'd seen it before on a torture victim who was trying to get a group together to force reform in his government.

"Where did you get those?"

"It's not important." He was getting his breath back. "I got in a jam overseas. They wanted information. I never gave it to them. They tried for two days."

"But they let you live?"

"I got rescued. Some people say I was lucky."

"So you don't think I've got the guts to make you talk."

"You might. But I have this strange reaction to pain. It makes me angry. I clam up. Could you do more to me than these people did?"

I untied him. What else could I do? "Real macho man," I muttered as he got up and rubbed his arms.

"You've got that wrong. I've never even fired a gun. Capturing you last night scared me to death."

"Why are you doing this? Who's paying you?"

"No one." His answer stumped me. People didn't make that kind of commitment without a payoff. He was probably lying.

"So where do we go from here?" I asked.

"We wait."

"And do what?"

"We could make friends with the dog. I take it nothing's actually wrong with him."

"My family is out there somewhere, stupid!" I shouted. "And I'm supposed to waste my time buddying up to a dog?"

Bob seemed taken aback. "Ben, I promise you, they're not in any physical danger. No one's hurting them or starving them. In fact, your boys are probably having the time of their lives."

"And Karen?"

"She won't be enjoying herself, but no one's hurting her. Believe me, okay?"

"What else can I do?" I said, more to myself than to him.

"No one's keeping you here. I threw the gun away, remember? If you don't want to trust me, you can always take a hike."

I stared at him, but he didn't blink. "You know I'll stay. But you're going to talk to me some time."

He made no promises. "We need to get to know the dog," he said after a moment of awkward silence. "He's not too effective if we have to keep him tied up."

"Effective against what?"

"Bears. Whatever."

"What're you hiding from me?"

He didn't answer, just went outside. I followed him, putting my sore arm back in the sling. He picked up an old cooking pot, opened a bin, and filled the pot with dog food and another with water from an outside tap. If he was still hurting, he gave no sign of it. Carefully he slid the food and water within range of the dog. Killer snarled at him but soon started to eat, crunching and slobbering over his food. He drank with heavy lapping sounds.

"Quite a dog," I admitted. The stark blackness of his hair made him more frightening than any shepherd I'd encountered.

"He's great. Just what we need."

"You're that afraid of bears?"

He ignored me and walked closer to Killer.

"You remember me?" Bob said, speaking to the dog. Killer lunged at him halfheartedly. Bob backed up a bit. "We met when I picked you out." Killer did not seem to appreciate the reminder.

I watched them for awhile. Bob really was serious about making friends with the dog, though I couldn't see the point. But then I couldn't see the point of anything that had happened. My family was missing, but Bob said they were okay but he didn't know where they were exactly but he knew what had happened to them but he refused to tell me. And here I was on the edge of the Canadian wilderness watching an unbalanced man try to get on the good side of a monster dog, and that man held the key to everything that mattered to me.

"So how long are we going to be here?" He paid no attention to me. "Bob?" I said, louder.

"What?"

"How long are we going to be here?"

"I don't know."

"That's it? You don't know? Give me an estimate — two days, a week, more?"

"I understand this is hard for you, Ben, but it's the best option we've got."

"Cut the platitudes," I said, the anger showing. "You don't have the slightest idea what I'm going through. Nothing you've said has given me any reason to trust you." I glared at him until he flinched. "Maybe I'm wasting my time."

"If you think so," he said evenly, "the road's down there. Cars go by once in awhile. You can hitch a ride."

"And then do what? Report it to the police? They'll just assume that Karen ran out on me. What evidence do I have that she didn't?"

"So you'll stay." He looked relieved.

"For now. But you better come up with some answers soon."

"There's no other way. You can't help Karen right now. Not without an army." He'd slipped again, and I could sense him cringing inside.

"She's kidnapped. That's what you're saying."

"Not exactly."

"Are the kids with her?"

"Probably not, but they're safe."

"Then why would we need an army?"

"Did I say army?"

I almost hit him again. The guy was a walking contradiction — tough looking on the outside and mush inside, but with a strange inner reserve, almost as if he dreamed of being a giant if he could only talk himself out of his fear. Clearly he would never tell me until he decided to. But it was obvious that he was afraid we'd be attacked. That's why he was chatting up the dog. I didn't have the heart to tell him the dog would calm down considerably anyway once we'd fed him for a couple of days.

"Look, Ben, I'm on your side. Really. We're here for good reasons."

"Which you won't reveal."

"No."

Lunch was a quiet affair. The only redeeming feature of the meal was that Bob wasn't a bad cook. The cabin was stocked with enough food for a few weeks, and Bob certainly knew what to do with it.

When we finished, I took another antibiotic pill, the second of the day. He watched me closely. "Those for your arm?"

"Yeah."

"How is it?"

"Okay, I hope. But unless you have some-

40

thing to replace the dressing with, I'd rather not take this one off to look."

"I don't. Is it stitched up?"

"Yeah. The antibiotics should do the trick. If it gets infected, I'll know it by the pain. What's the matter, Bob? You afraid I'll wimp out if we have to fight?"

"Fight who?"

"The people you think are on their way."

"You're dreaming."

"No, I'm not. And guess what, Bob — neither of us are fighters. You better pray Killer knows what he's doing."

"Nobody's coming after us. We left those two guys behind at McDonald's."

"Says you. All right, what about basic living arrangements? We left our suitcases in the other car. My car. What do we do for clothes, shaving gear . . ."

"There's no one here but us, Ben. We can wash out a few things. Beards are in these days."

"You're lucky I had my pills in my jacket."

"What about the stitches? When are they supposed to come out?"

"A week or so. I can snip them myself if I have to."

"Then we're all set."

"You ever read *Alice in Wonderland*?"

"No. Why?"

"I figured that must be where you are. You certainly aren't living in this dimension." He looked away, and I pressed him: "Unless you start leveling with me —"

"I know, but I can't. Not yet."

"You're scared out of your wits and you're in way over your head. As near as I can see you either got suckered into it for the money or you're working for Karen. If it's Karen, she doesn't have any money. Maybe you've got another reason for doing her this kind of favor."

"What makes you think it's Karen?"

"The note. You said it was a signal for you. The reference to the cat we don't have."

"All right, I'm doing it for Karen. We pre-arranged a signal for her to put in the note. But there's nothing between us."

"Where'd you meet her?"

"At church."

"So you're a Bible thumper, like her." It was becoming plainer. "For a Bible thumper, you've done some pretty naughty things lately holding me up with a gun —"

"Fake gun," he broke in, embarrassed.

"— lying to a border guard," I went on. "Who knows what else."

"I'm not proud of it."

"What's Karen's plan? Where did she go? Where are my kids?"

Then it was like a curtain drew across his face. He wasn't going to tell me because Karen didn't want me to know. And I still had nothing. Here I was, with my family only God knew where, and I was still too far from the truth to do anything about it.

FOUR

By evening we had settled into a prickly routine. Bob cooked because he was better at it, and I cleaned up. We both spent time sitting and staring. I had my reasons, but I could only guess at Bob's. He looked troubled, and several times an hour he would go to the window and stare down the hill to the driveway entrance and the road.

Later he turned on the television. Reception was bad, but he got a news program. I suppose it was inevitable, though I was surprised by the speed of it: Someone had traced down my car, and I'd become a missing person. My bosses, no doubt. They were paranoid about their talented staff (or about the information those staff had stored in their inflated crania).

So a hue and cry had gone out. The monastery had been contacted, but they, of course, knew nothing about me. Foul play was not suspected at this time, but anyone knowing the whereabouts, et cetera, et cetera. I wondered what they'd do with my half-paid-for car. Just at the end of the cov-

44

erage, the story mentioned that my house had also been abandoned. Neighbors had reported a large white, unmarked truck that had loaded up the furniture. My wife had been seen directing the movers . . .

I clicked off the set. "Any of this interesting to you, Bob?"

"Some." He shifted in his chair.

"She went voluntarily."

"Looks like it."

"Was she running out on me?"

He looked at the floor, pondering the design in the worn rug. Then he gave me a level gaze and said, "No."

We both sat in silence for awhile until Bob stood and walked to the front window. "We can't keep this up," he said. "There are things I'm not supposed to tell you, things Karen doesn't want me to tell you. You'll have to trust me like I trust her."

"And if you're lying?"

"Why would I? You've seen that I'm no professional kidnapper."

"You're selling yourself short, Bob. Here I am, eating right out of your hand. Everything you wanted to do with me has happened." But I didn't believe he was working for some kind of mob. He could see in my eyes that I didn't. Bob was too unstable for the kind of work tough guys would find useful.

"Can we get off this, Ben? Why don't you tell me about yourself."

"Maybe I don't want to get that chummy. I've got other things on my mind."

"Karen told me you work for some kind of political consulting firm?" he said, ignoring my objection.

I gave up. There was nothing I could do about Karen right then anyway. "Libertec. That's the company I work for. But I'm not supposed to talk about it except when I'm with the in-crowd."

"Your background then."

"Simple stuff. Raised in Arizona. High school track star — that was my fifteen minutes of fame. Eventually I got a masters degree in poli-sci and Libertec recruited me."

"Are you still fast?"

"Pardon me?"

"Do you stay in shape? Running?"

"Yeah. Old Speedy Sylvester himself."

Bob seemed to be taking a mental note of that one. "Did Libertec give you any self-defense training, like . . . I don't know . . . like spies get?"

"Spies are for Deighton novels. Most of the people you think of as spies are just collectors and sorters of information. I've only been in one hand-to-hand fight in my life and that was when Sammy Lester stole my candy bar in elementary school."

"And the fight where you got the knife in the arm," he said, pointing to my sling.

"That one too, but it wasn't much of a battle. I saved my neck by fleeing the scene."

"Where'd you meet Karen?"

"UCLA, when I was going for my masters. She was an undergrad in fine arts. I knocked her down in my hurry to get to a class."

"Some introduction to a romance."

"It gets worse. She broke her arm. I spent so much time apologizing in between paying off her medical bills, she started feeling sorry for me."

I decided to turn the tables. "Why don't you tell me about those burn scars on your chest."

He hesitated, but it was obvious that, for whatever reason, he wanted to build bridges between us. "I was working in the Far East — Thailand."

"What kind of work?"

"It doesn't matter."

"Hey, I thought you wanted to be my buddy. How can we be friends if we don't share our innermost secrets?"

"I'm a librarian."

"A what?" I stifled a laugh. "You pulled off this stunt, and you're a librarian?"

"I also work out regularly and run a six-minute mile. You want to hear my story or not?"

"Shoot."

"I'd been working in the public library system in Denver, getting bored, when I heard about a job in Thailand, a recon project."

"What's that?"

"Computer reconversion of a catalog. It was for a university department that taught English language and literature. Everything was going fine until the day I witnessed a shooting. A prominent guy in the drug scene bought the farm right in front of me. The police questioned me, but the dead guy's pals wanted to do their own investigation. They figured I could identify the man with the gun."

"So they snatched you."

"Next day, right off the sidewalk and into a car. They took me to a run-down house in the jungle and started the burning cigarette routine."

"It didn't work, because you didn't know anything."

"It didn't work because I wouldn't tell them. I'd recognized the killer. He had a stall in the market — sold hand tools. My torturers weren't smart enough to figure out

48

that I'd already given the police enough information to lock the shooter away where the avengers couldn't reach him."

"So why didn't you talk?"

"Because then they would have won." He said it quietly.

I looked at him with new appreciation. "Pretty stupid of you."

"I know."

"So what happened?"

"When the police came to my house to take me to ID the guy they'd arrested, I wasn't around. They made some inquiries and someone tipped them off. When they burst into the house where I was being held, they nearly blew my head off before they got the bad guys. I quit my job and came home."

He paused, staring blankly for a few seconds. "It sounds simple in the telling, but it left me with what they call Post-Traumatic Stress Disorder. I was mostly a basket case for a few months."

"You must have recovered. Look how sane you are now."

"I found a job in a public library in Bellingham. I was a real mess, but I guess they saw a spark of life somewhere." He grinned awkwardly. I hated to admit it, but I was starting to like this character.

"You're cured now?"

A strange light came into his eyes, and he paused as if going over it in his mind before he spoke. "I think the word is *revolutionized*." He looked at me with hesitation on his face. "I don't know how a guy like you will relate to this, but when I moved to Lynden I could hardly go out the door every morning and get into my car. So I figured that since church was for cripples, I better go there."

"And you had a life-changing encounter with Jesus," I said, a mockingly hard edge to my voice.

He got up. "I don't know about you, but I'm bushed. Maybe it's all that bruising from the two-by-four you used on me. You sure pack a wallop."

Guilt's an unpleasant thing. For a minute I almost apologized for making fun of his faith, even for hurting him earlier. But this guy had a lot of explanations to make before I was ready to put him on the side of the angels. I mumbled a goodnight and headed for my room. For awhile, I looked out into the darkness, sensing but not quite seeing the mountain across the valley. The whole situation was still too bizarre for me to handle. Here I was buried in a quagmire of uncertainty, in limbo, locked into a symbiotic relationship with a not-so-tough librarian who still held all the cards.

And all around me was wilderness.

I slept uneasily, dreaming of Karen in trouble, calling to me, the two boys in trouble, calling to me, and I was chained to a wall with Bob standing there laughing, dangling the keys in front of my face. Then the chains disappeared, but I was still stuck to the wall as if I were incapable of removing myself.

"Prisoner Ben," someone said. "Ladies and gentlemen, please acknowledge Prisoner Ben." And I saw a large crowd of beaming folks in the midst of a tour, with me as the main attraction. I shouted to them, begging them to help me get free so that I could get to Karen and the kids. But they seemed to think I wanted to be there, pinned to the wall, as if I had chosen it.

I awoke sweating, hoping I hadn't called out in my sleep, wondering how long my sanity could hold. One thing was clear — I had to get control of this situation. Whatever I did, I had to nurture a hatred of Bob.

He probably wondered at my coldness while we ate breakfast in silence, but he gave no sign of it. My mood was sullen, watchful. There had to be a way to get into his head and pull out the information I needed. Maybe torture wouldn't do it, but somehow there had to be a key to unlock Bob.

That morning we untied the dog. Killer was greatly subdued, recognizing for good or for ill that we were his meal ticket. He still wouldn't let us pet him, but he didn't sink his teeth into anyone's leg either.

I began to pay closer attention to the property we were on. The front couple of acres, facing the road, were far lower than the back eight. The driveway climbed a good sixty vertical feet to a plateau where the cabin was. From the living room window we could see the first third of the driveway and some of the paved road. There was no other car access to the property.

For lack of anything better to do, we took Killer for a walk in the woods. The big cedars blocked out enough of the sun to make the undergrowth sparse, so getting around was fairly easy. Trails had been cut and maintained. If I hadn't been so tense about Karen and the kids, I might have enjoyed it.

After about half an hour, Bob murmured, "We shouldn't be gone too long," and headed back. I followed him, sheep-like, not really caring much. As I walked behind him, I marveled at how easy it would be to pick up a rock and end his miserable existence. But I resisted, angry at myself that we were starting to treat each other with consideration and respect.

What did I know about him except that he was supposedly acting as Karen's agent? Even if he was working on Karen's behalf, he must have realized that hiding crucial information from me made no sense. How could I help her if I had no idea what had happened?

If Bob was acting for Karen, there had to be a reason for him to hide me in the loneliest place on earth. It could have been that he was waiting for instructions, but why not hold me prisoner in my own home? Why drag me into the wilderness?

In my mind, I started organizing the facts: Karen was gone; the kids were gone. She'd left a note with a signal in it. I'd been kidnapped by some nut who took me to a cabin in Canada. He was obviously an amateur at this sort of thing, and he'd told me he was working for Karen. I had to admit that I believed him.

I'm not sure how the thought finally came to me, but when it did my mind couldn't get around it. There was only one possible explanation that could fit the situation, but it was crazy. For some unknown reason, Karen must have told Bob to take me out of the action, to put me in limbo. Karen wanted me kidnapped? She wanted me isolated in a cabin in a Canadian forest, with no means to come after her?

How could that be? If she was in trouble, I should have been searching for her, trying to rescue her. What reason could she have to neutralize me? She'd left the note with the reference to the phony cat. Why tell me that and then prevent me from helping her?

Did she believe she could solve whatever it was by herself? Or was it so bad that she'd given up hope of getting out of it and wanted to make sure I didn't get sucked into it too?

No, it was impossible. We loved each other, and if someone had done something to her and the boys, she'd want me to move mountains to reach her. We loved our kids, and we had every reason to protect them. It made no sense for Karen to go to all this trouble, planned out in advance, just to take me out of the action.

But every other explanation I tried fell apart. As senseless as it was, there was no other way to fit the pieces together. Karen — my mind stumbled at the thought — Karen had told Bob to put me somewhere where I couldn't even make an attempt to find her.

But I wasn't going to do what she wanted, whatever her reason. I was going to find her and the kids.

I watched Bob ahead of me, and for a crazy moment I tried to project my mind into his, as if I could pull his knowledge out of his head. I needed a break in our impasse, some shift in the circumstances that would get things moving. Where it would come from, I had no idea, but I was not going to tolerate this futility much longer.

I watched Killer, calm, watchful as he walked through the woods, a beast who was controlled by no one and who protected with force the territory he called his own. Even though he was frightening, the dog brought his own brand of security. If it was true that we were in danger, a danger Bob refused to admit, I was prepared to count on Killer.

The air was chilly as we came out of the woods. A breeze carried with it damp, cold air that held a promise of snow, maybe not right away, but within the next few weeks for sure.

Bob looked uneasy, his tension clearly having grown through the afternoon. That evening he was unbearable — pacing, shifting in his chair, getting up to look out the window. He made me nervous. Later Bob got some long nails out of a drawer, and I heard him hammering on the front porch. When he came in, he had a look of satisfaction on his face.

"What were you doing?"

"I got a piece of thick plywood and hammered some spikes through it."

"What for?"

"A little extra protection outside the door. I saw it in a movie. Sort of a deadly welcome mat."

"And just who are you expecting?" He didn't answer. "Just remind me before I go outside in the morning," I told him. "A nail through the foot would really make my day."

FIVE

They came in the early hours, maybe two or two-thirty. Because I was sleeping restlessly, feeding on a tension that was far from nameless, Killer's barking put me bolt awake. I crept into Bob's room in the dark and shook him.

Killer was roaring now, full-throated and dangerous, obviously trying to drive something or someone away. We waited, not sure what to do, both of us counting on the dog to solve the problem for us. Then there was a single gunshot and silence. I felt sick.

If there were two or more of them, they'd probably come in opposite doors and try to trap us in the middle. The cabin was built on simple lines — a rectangle with a middle hallway and doors at each end.

"What should we do?" Bob whispered.

"Get out if we can," I told him. "I for one am not going to wait for them to blow my head off at close range."

"If we run for it, they'll shoot us."

"If that's what they're here for, they'll probably shoot us anyway."

"Where can we go?"

"Do you have the car keys?" I asked.

"Yeah." He fumbled for them on the dresser. "Here."

"Whoever comes in the back door will be in a narrow hall. The second the door opens, we'll charge him. If we can take him out, maybe we can find out from him who else is out there, deal with him, and get the car going."

"What if there are three or more?"

"Then we're dead."

"Maybe someone will come in the front door while we're waiting at the back."

"It's locked. This one isn't. And you left a welcome mat, remember?"

We waited. They were taking their time, maybe hoping we hadn't heard the commotion. The gunshot had been low caliber, not very loud. Even if we had heard it, they had some hope we'd come out to see what was happening. Then we'd be sitting ducks. There was no sound from Killer, no sound of anything except our breathing.

The first sign was a creak on the back stairs. There were four steps, I remembered. We held our breaths as the guy moved up them. The handle turned — the door had no lock on it. Bob waited in a bedroom doorway on one side of the hall. I was behind the door. Slowly it opened inward. Counting on the guy to hang onto the knob, I let him open the door about a foot and then I grabbed the handle and yanked it inward — hard.

He came with it, stumbling into the hall, his head lowered at just the right angle for Bob to slug him in the back of the neck. I stuck out a foot, and he went down. Distantly I heard the sound of a male scream — Bob's welcome mat at the other door. We had some time.

"Get the gun!" I shouted, grabbing the guy's other arm and kneeling on his back. Bob wrestled the small pistol out of his hand and we both got up fast. Our invader lay there for a second, then rose halfway before he saw the gun leveled at his head. Bob was good at pretending he knew how to handle firearms.

The man was short, wiry, dressed in black. He was furious, but we had no time for that. We herded him into a bedroom, and I tied him up with a couple of pillowcases while Bob held the gun. Then I turned him face up on the bed. He knew what was coming and looked suitably scared.

"How many others are there?" I asked. He hesitated only a second before Bob rapped him smartly on one shin with the gun. The guy yelled. I patted him on the shoulder. "My friend here is a little anxious to hear what you have to say." When there was no answer, Bob hit him on the other shin, then the first one for good measure. I looked at Bob in surprise. He shrugged, the pistol bobbing.

"There's one more." The guy was squinting and tears were starting to run down his face.

"Where is he?"

"Other door. Should have been in by now."

In answer, there was a crash at the other end of the house, then another and the sound of splintering wood. We ran for the door in time to see a man come through it, fragments flying. He half fell on the other side, and as he scrambled up, Bob faced him with the gun.

This guy was a cool one. He ignored the pistol, gave up his own to Bob who put it in his pocket, sat down on the linoleum, and pulled off one shoe, revealing two splotches of blood on the bottom of his foot. "Dirty pool," he muttered. "You two were supposed to be pushovers."

"So why have we got the gun while you're sitting on the floor?" Bob said. I tried to signal him with my eyes not to get too cocky.

The cool one glared at him. "Okay, you've got me," he said. "Did you put poison on the nails?"

"No. Were you worried?"

"Just wondering about infection. You got anything for it? I don't want a case of blood poisoning."

"Why should we help you? It's just a few puncture wounds." But Bob was starting to look uncertain.

"What does it matter?" I said. "Anything to keep the guy from whining."

I went to get some disinfectant in the bathroom, trusting Bob to stay alert. When I got back, I opened the bottle, handing it down to the guy on the floor. He grabbed it and blasted about half the bottle right back into my face, then sprang at Bob with a speed I could hardly believe. But Bob saw him coming and whacked him on the side of the head with the gun. Bob told me this later, because I was already on my way to the kitchen sink to wash out my eyes. They'd be bloodshot for a week.

When I got back, blinking and seeing everything through a fuzzy haze, the guy was conscious, holding his head and groaning.

"What now?" I asked Bob.

"We question them. I need to know more."

"I thought you knew it all, Bob."

"Not by half. Karen was afraid this might happen."

"So were you."

"Yeah, well, let's get on with it."

We dragged the injured guy into the back bedroom and tied him up beside his buddy. Then, going to the kitchen, we held a conference.

"I'm getting squeamish about this, Ben."

"Why? You seemed to enjoy bashing the other guy's shins."

"Is that what you think? That I'm getting some sort of rush out of playing the heavy?"

"Yes." He didn't take it very well, frowning, shaking his head. "You want me to do the next bit?" I asked.

"No. I know what I need to find out. You don't."

"I've still got the car keys. When we're done with these two, we'll have to find somewhere else. Any ideas?"

"Sure," he said, but he was distracted. "Let's do this part first."

We went back into the bedroom. Our attackers looked pathetic, lying side by side, trussed up like calves at a rodeo. "Which one?" I asked Bob.

"The little guy. He's got a nicer singing voice." For someone feeling squeamish, Bob sounded pretty pumped up to me. "First question: Who sent you?"

The guy, shorter than the other one by six inches, looked at his partner, terror in his eyes. The cool one showed no emotion.

"I'm not talking to your pal," Bob said evenly. "I'm asking you."

"Nobody sent us. We were driving by and decided to rob you."

"Wrong answer." Bob slapped him on the shin again with the gun. By my count that was three times on that leg.

"He'll kill me," the guy protested, pain standing out in his eyes.

"Who? Your friend here?"

"Him too. I'm not talking." Whack. That was the second one on the other leg. One more would make a match. The little guy obviously was thinking along the same lines, because he started babbling.

"We work for a guy named Hans. We do jobs. I don't know anything else. Please don't hit me again."

"Hans who?"

"Blocker. Works out of Seattle."

"What was your job here?"

"To do him." The guy waved his chin in my direction. "And anybody with him."

"To kill us?"

"Yeah." The cool one beside him grunted deep in his throat.

"Why?" I asked.

"I don't know." Bob raised the gun barrel again.

"Honest. Nobody told me —"

He got no chance to finish. A voice behind us said, "Give me the gun." Bob turned quickly, raising the pistol. Then he stopped, his hand dropping, the light going out of his eyes.

A man, large, hard, stood in the doorway. He was holding what looked like an Uzi. As he stepped forward into the light, I stared at the ice blue eyes and the rough beard. A man to be reckoned with. "Untie them." His voice was low, husky. He motioned for Bob to give him the pistol, and the one bulging in his pocket.

We untied our captives. As soon as the little guy was free, he swung at Bob, sending him reeling. "Stop that!" the big man barked. The other two didn't exactly stand at attention, but they came close. Obviously, this was Hans. They backed off and waited at one side of the room. Hans gave them back their guns.

"What do you people want?" I heard myself saying. I hoped the terror didn't show too much in my voice. The question was futile anyway. We all knew what they were planning.

"We've got a job to finish," Hans said, his face expressionless. "Which one of you has the keys to the car out there?" I turned them over to him. "We sit tight until morning," Hans said, seemingly distracted. "Then we'll go for a drive."

He made us sit on the sofa in the front room while one or other of the three of them kept a gun on us at all times. I was kicking myself for not suspecting that there was a third guy. With two of us to take out, the opposition would have been bound to stack the deck in its favor.

The little guy with the bruised shins kept glaring at Bob. The cool one spent a long time doctoring his punctured foot. I hoped his tetanus shots weren't up to date. Hans just sat and stared, preoccupied no doubt with the plans for our demise. The only glimmer of hope I could see was that they hadn't shot us yet. This probably meant they were planning a convenient accident so that no one would suspect we'd been murdered. But I, for one, wasn't planning to cooperate. There's something about facing certain death that makes you more open to thinking about risky possibilities.

It was a long night. Though I dozed occasionally, I spent a lot of time thinking about Karen and the kids. I'd passed the point of feeling blind panic for them, and now there was only a coldness in the pit of my stomach. If a hit had been put out on me, I had little hope that my family would be spared either. But for the ever-shortening life of me, I could not understand why anyone would do this to us. The only person who hated me enough was Karen's father, and he wouldn't kidnap his own daughter, would he?

I remembered the first time I'd met Jim Barker. Power oozed out of the guy in unlimited supply and struck down anyone in a ten-foot radius. He was used to getting what he wanted. That's how he'd built up an enormous electronics conglomerate with tentacles and government contracts all over the world.

He'd massacred Karen. What she could have been without him dominating everything she ever did, I didn't know. He'd been apoplectic when he found out we eloped, and she'd been so scared of what he'd do that she wouldn't stay alone in our apartment for the first six months of our marriage. I took her everywhere or left her with friends. After we moved to Lynden, she settled down, but I still couldn't reach the Karen locked inside her, no matter how close we got.

Her loving dad had cut her off. He wrote her out of his will. For the first year after we were married, the only contact she had with her parents was a few letters from her mother through a sympathetic third party. Then he started phoning her regularly, but only to convince her to dump me and take over the company when he retired. Karen told me he had groomed her all her life to replace him. He'd taught her business and management at home and insisted that she major in the sciences in high school. Unable to fight him, she'd died inside, or better still, she'd developed a cold shell around a core of fear. Heaven only knows how she got the courage to drop her engineering major at university and take up fine arts. She never told him what she'd done.

I stretched out an arm, and the little guy whose turn it was to guard us shook his gun at me as if to reassure me that I was still his prisoner. Bob was asleep, his head lolling sideways. The guy never ceased to amaze me. Feeling weary myself, I leaned my head back and started to drift.

"Wake him up." My head jerked at the sudden sound, and I realized I'd been sleeping. Hans had walked into the room, soundless, like a cougar on the prowl. I shook Bob, and he cried out, blinking, his face a mask of terror.

"It's okay, Bob," I said.

He looked embarrassed as he took in his surroundings. "Must have fallen asleep."

"We've got work to do," Hans said, his voice flat. "You guys have any hiking boots?"

"Why? Are we going on a nature walk?" I asked, testing his mood. He walked over and backhanded me across the face. My head exploded in a mass of silvery stars, and I tasted blood.

"Hiking boots?" he repeated.

"No. There are a couple of pairs of rubbers over there that might fit us." My words were slurred, the right side of my face already starting to swell.

"Put them on. Your coats too." We obeyed, neither of us looking at the other, avoiding the fear we knew we'd see in one another's eyes. As we went down the back steps, I saw a dark shape spread out at the other end of the lawn. Killer. He wasn't moving.

SIX

"What's Cascade Falls?" Bob and I were alone in his borrowed car, with me driving. Our executioners were behind us in a small four-by-four because Hans had insisted that the three of them stay out of our car so that forensics wouldn't find anything suspicious. For my part, I didn't like the sound of the word *forensics*.

"It's a regional park with a waterfall," Bob told me. "Terrain's pretty rugged. They've put in some trails and wooden stairs so that people can get a photo of the falls without breaking their necks."

"What kind of accident could we have there?"

"You name it." Bob thought for a moment. "It seems to me they'd build on the climbing angle. The safe areas are fenced, but some people like to be close to the action. They get a rush out of climbing spray-covered rocks."

"A person could have a nasty fall?"

"No doubt about it. By the time you went over the falls and got carried down the rapids below it . . ." He paused. I could tell he saw no way out of this. It was ultimate reality time. "Ben?" he said, and I knew what was coming.

"Save it," I told him. "If you've got a faith for moments like these, more power to you. But I plan to leave this world under my own steam, and I don't expect to pick up a harp on the other side."

We drove in silence for a few minutes, my words of bravado contradicted by the hammering of my heart. The park turnoff appeared, and I knew it was time to get my plan into gear. We had no weapons, only the car, but I was good, and this Honda would be perfect if I could get the right conditions operating.

"Tell me about the road in," I said. "Are there any long steep parts?"

"There are two parking lots, one at the bottom and the other at the end of a steep hill."

"Is the road narrow?"

"Yes."

"Does it go farther?"

"It's part of a logging road that runs way up into the hills."

We rounded the corner, and I spotted the first parking lot. Instead of stopping, I booted the car up the rough incline that led to the second lot. Hans started blowing the horn behind me, but it didn't matter. Nothing mattered but speed.

The upper parking lot, when we reached it, was gravel, and I did a fast one-eighty so that we faced the way we'd come. Perfect. I wouldn't need the higher part of the road. The four-by-four was a hundred feet back down the road when I hit the gas and drove at it head on. There's something terrifically liberating about being a condemned man. Hans must have realized that in the game of chicken, the one with nothing to lose always wins.

At the last possible second, the four-by-four veered over the bank, slid a few feet, then started to roll. It did two complete revolutions before it smacked into a tree. We slowed to watch the show then floored it out of there, Bob shouting while I blew the horn insanely. No shots were fired. Our would-be executioners were too shaken up to do anything as we left the park and headed back down Sylvester Road.

We stopped at the cabin long enough to grab a few things. I wanted to bury Killer, but Bob warned me that Hans and his crew would probably soon hitch a ride out of the park and be back on our trail.

What puzzled me was how they had found

us so easily. I went to the car, crouched down, and started feeling around the edge of the underside. In two or three minutes I found it — a small black box.

"What's that?" Bob asked.

"Homing device," I told him.

"How did it get there?"

"Someone left the car for you to pick up at McDonald's, right?"

"Sure, but no one outside our circle knew I'd even be involved with you or that we'd be switching cars."

"We know there were two guys waiting for us beside my car. What if the third guy followed us into McDonald's and stayed behind us when we went outside? It was dark. He could have run in at a low crouch and planted the box without us knowing."

"Why would he have a homing device on him?"

"I don't know. Maybe his involvement in the Boy Scouts taught him always to be prepared." I looked closer at the device, my eyes resting on some small raised lettering on one corner. Bob heard my breath suddenly suck in and he crowded close to have a look. The homer was made by Barker Electronics, the company owned by my father-in-law. Just a coincidence?

We got into the car and headed toward

Mission. I let Bob drive and spent the next ten minutes or so thinking, before I made up my mind.

"There's only one explanation that fits, Bob," I said carefully.

"Explanation for what?"

"This whole miserable episode of my life. I know who took Karen and sent those goons after us — my father-in-law."

Bob said nothing, just stared at the winding road ahead of him. My anger had never stopped simmering below the surface, and I heard myself shouting at him, "Did you already know that, Bob?"

"I didn't know they planned to kill you. And what makes you think it's Jim Barker anyway?"

"He gave them a homer made in his own factory."

"It's a big company. The homer could be coincidence."

"And Karen left home voluntarily. The news story said the neighbors watched her directing the moving truck. She would have fought like a bag of wet cats if some stranger was snatching her. It had to be her dad." He didn't answer me. I sensed words were bubbling below the surface, but nothing came out.

Slowly we drove down the main street of

Mission. "Where are we going?" I muttered, scarcely caring. I was tired, and my mind did not want to take in any more deceptions. Instead of answering, Bob turned right at Grand Avenue, just past a movie theater, and went up a steep hill. I counted the numbered streets — Second, Third. At Seventh, we came to a stop sign, then went a few more blocks, turning right at a road fronting a large city park. Bob pulled in and stopped.

"Are we going to camp by the swings?" I asked, goading him.

Bob looked grieved, then shook his head and got out. We walked along winding sidewalks through the green area, Bob saying nothing. Finally he dropped onto a bench. The air was colder than it had been, but there was still no rain.

He hesitated for a few seconds before he said, "Did you see whether they were all right?"

"Who?"

"Hans and his goons."

"Who cares?"

"I do."

I stared at him in disbelief. Then, in utter frustration, I stood and walked back to the car. He had to run to catch up. Why I was blessed with such a bleeding heart I'll never know. One minute he was bashing people with his pistol barrel and the next he was wondering if they'd bruised themselves in their nasty fall.

Just before we reached the car, I stopped short and faced him. "If you want to care about someone, why not choose me for once? What right did you have to keep secrets from me and risk my life? If you knew about Hans and his boys, why didn't you tell me?"

"I had no idea who they were or that they wanted to kill you."

"What did you think they were programmed to do?"

"To keep you away from Karen. At the worst, they might rough you up a bit. I never dreamed they'd be executioners."

"Why does Jim Barker want me dead?"

"I can't tell you." I grabbed him by the collar and squeezed a bit, then let him go. This was useless.

"Did Jim Barker take Karen?"

"Yes. As far as I know."

"You knew it all along." He looked away. "What does he want? Is this some plot to wreck our marriage? If so, why's he doing it now?"

Bob opened the car door on the passenger side and got in. "We've got to get rid of the homer." A chilly wind had started to blow, and I felt the cold deep inside. The clouds were uniform gray, constantly threatening rain. I sensed my anger turning from Bob onto the man who deserved it most — my father-in-law.

"Where to?" I said.

"We need to put the homer on some vehicle that moves around a lot — a bus or a taxi."

"Why not just smash the thing?"

"If we keep it alive, we might be able to throw them off the trail. Head down the hill and turn left at Second." I did what I was told. We passed a museum and a library. Just beyond the library was a bus stop with a bus in front of it, Cascade something on the side.

"Where does it go?"

"It's inter-city," Bob told me. "Goes to Vancouver and back to Harrison." He wasn't dumb. If Hans and his crew had survived their crash — and I was sure they had — it might take them days to realize they were following a bus.

We parked, and Bob sauntered across the street. Alongside the big vehicle he stooped to tie a shoelace and snapped the homer to the underside, its strong magnet gripping the metal. We were set.

"What now?" I asked, hating to sound helpless. But Bob was the only one of us who knew his way around.

"Lunch," he said. "How about a fish and chip place near the mall?"

"Okay."

We found a corner table and ate an uneasy meal. The effects of our morning were becoming plain, and fish and chips turned out to be a bad choice for queasy stomachs. While we ate, Bob laid out his plans.

"First Hans and company. Unless you killed them —"

"Which I didn't," I interjected.

"— they'll be following the homer. We have anywhere from a few hours to a couple of days to get well hidden."

"I don't care what you do," I told him. "I'm going after Jim Barker. No more hiding."

"We're both going after Jim Barker, but we're going to do it my way."

"Why should we?"

"Because I know what to do and you don't."

"If you know what you're doing, what was that vacation up Sylvester Road that nearly got us killed?"

"Karen's idea. But now since you've figured out most of it, we're moving to Plan B."

I picked up another fry and grimaced. My

appetite was shot to pieces. What bothered me even more was that Bob was still in charge. This was definitely not the way I wanted it, being led around by a crazy.

"Do you have any idea what Plan B is?" I asked him.

"Sure. It's all worked out."

"Do I go into hiding again, or are we finally going to do something?"

"I'm going to do something. You're going to hide. Sorry."

"And if I just walk out of here?"

"You'll probably never find Karen, and Hans will take you out within a week."

"What can you give me to prove you've actually got a strategy worked out? Maybe I'm better off on my own."

"I don't have anything. You have to trust me."

"I did trust you. It's only because I took charge that we're not dead."

"Know what I think, Ben?" I didn't respond. "You'd have trouble trusting the Pope."

"Are you a shrink too?"

"You're just dying for a chance to take control and save your woman."

"Don't forget my kids," I sneered, hating him.

"Why not? You forget them all the time.

I've heard lots of concern about Karen, but you've hardly said boo about your children."

"Why the sudden hostility?" I asked evenly, controlling my temper. He backed off and made an apologetic gesture with his hand. "Pressure getting to you? Are you spooked because you're not used to looking death in the face? I thought you couldn't wait for the blessed moment when you could rest in the arms of Jesus forever."

He had no idea how to react to me. I saw anger, confusion, and hurt on his face. "I'm sorry," he said. "It gets a little tough sometimes to stomach your sarcasm. You must be proud of the way you've cornered the market on hate."

"You sound like a soap opera, Bob." We were both seething, a reaction to the events of the past several hours.

"My name's not Bob."

"Oh. Revelation time. So what did your mother really call you?"

"Jeff."

"As in Mutt and Jeff?"

"Cute."

"What's the rest of it?"

"Jeff Mancuso."

"Is that supposed to mean something to me?"

"No."

"Then why not tell me your real name from the beginning?"

"I wanted to see how things were shaping up first. There was no good reason for me to trust you either."

I pushed back from the table and got up. "Seems like we've formed a pretty good mutual hate-hate society," I muttered.

"We better move on."

"Where to, Jeff?" I asked, eyeing him warily as he stood.

"To see my brother. If you liked me, wait till you meet him."

SEVEN

The house was modest, post-war and gray, though it was obvious, even in November, that someone had done a great deal of landscaping. For myself, I was feeling so shell-shocked that I would not have been awed by a five-star hotel or dismayed by a lean-to in the woods. We were entering a new phase, and I'd probably find out more about Karen, but I was too numb to appreciate it. All I could think of was a warm bed and some freedom from Bob — no, Jeff.

But it was not to be. Here we were at the house of strangers, and goodness knows what waited for me inside. Jeff wouldn't tell me, though he seemed confident, even plucky, as he walked up the sidewalk and rang the bell. It was clear from the moment the door opened that he'd planned his strategy some time before. The man who greeted us could have been a clone of Jeff, only older. Solid, same curly hair, strong face, square jaw.

"Is this him?" he asked Jeff, who nodded. "Were you followed?"

"Take it easy, Dave," Jeff told him. "Everything's under control." He turned to me. "Ben, meet my brother Dave — Reverend David Mancuso."

Great, I told myself. A man of the cloth. Brother to the lunatic. This was shaping up to be worse than I feared. He even smiled like Jeff.

"Could I talk to you, Jeff?" I said as we stood on the doorstep.

"Why?" he asked.

"Humor me."

Jeff looked uneasily at his brother. "Dave, I'm . . ."

"Go ahead," Dave said. "I'll wait for you inside."

When the door closed, I grabbed his shoulder. "Are you crazy involving your family in this? People are trying to kill me."

"My family's been involved a long time. Dave owns the cabin, and the car for that matter. I rented the dog from a junkyard. That's going to cost me. Dave was feeding him while we waited for you to show up from your overseas trip."

I looked at him, pondering. "You're going to have to tell me all of it. No more secrets."

"That's why we're here."

They took me through the routine of properly meeting Dave and his wife Edith, a warm though slightly worried looking woman, slim, brown hair beginning to gray. Their home was lower middle class, pleasant, nothing out of taste, but nothing daring either. This couple was not in any kind of adventure mode.

"We're glad to have you stay with us for awhile," Edith said, her smile natural.

I said something or other, hopefully polite, while at the same time looking quizzically at Jeff. Maybe there was resentment in the look. My life was once again being planned for me so that I was unable to take any initiative. Karen and the kids could have been on the moon and it wouldn't have been harder for me to find them.

We went through supper, small talk. I was starting to seethe. It was like watching Nero fiddle while Rome burned and having everyone around me refuse to pass me a bucket. I watched the bland faces of Dave and Edith, the indecipherable face of Jeff, and I craved authority, control, knowledge. I wanted to be rid of the pack of them and on my way to Karen.

What I soon found out was that the situation was a lot more complicated than I thought. Jeff, looking slightly smug, broached the subject after supper: "Okay, Ben, it's time to tell all."

"Like at the end of a Sherlock Holmes movie?"

"Not exactly. Dave's got the video set up in a spare room so you can have some privacy."

"What am I watching — *Star Trek Fourteen*?"

"No. Karen." He led me into a room where a video was set up. To tell the truth, I had no idea what I was about to see. Maybe there was no way to prepare for it. Jeff went out, closing the door behind him. I turned it on.

She was wearing her favorite outfit, looking like a fashion model. I couldn't tell from the background where it had been taken, but there was no doubt that it was Karen on the color screen in front of me.

"Hi, Ben," she said. I tried to read her expression but couldn't be sure. "This thing makes me nervous." She smiled hesitantly. "If you're watching this now, it means that Jeff wasn't able to convince you that I'd left voluntarily, and that you're champing at the bit to find me." She paused awkwardly. "It also means I didn't get away in time. In that case, I'll have left a note with a reference to a cat."

"Yes, you did," I murmured.

"I've got lots to explain, and now that I'm

doing it there's too much to tell you. Where should I start?"

"At the beginning," I told her. "I need answers."

But she was going on. "You know about my involvement with the church, but I haven't been telling you things. I'm sorry for that now. It's just that I had to be sure. I am now. Ben" — she looked right into my soul — "I met God."

There was something different about her eyes. I'd never known someone with Alzheimer's, but it must be something like that — the body's the same but the person inside is a stranger. And the Karen I knew, or half knew, was hardly there anymore. The words she was speaking went right past me, as if she'd become a mystic forbidden to say anything but nonsense.

I rewound the machine back to the words, "I met God," and forced myself to listen. She was articulate. "I've lived most of my life under the cloud of someone else's dream. From the earliest I remember, he's charted it all out for me — daddy's little executive in training, getting set to take over the business. There was no reasoning with him; you know that."

I knew. Jim Barker lived in a world where anyone who disagreed with him was either an idiot or an enemy. He was always so right, always had all the reasons ready at the tip of his ever-smooth tongue. There was no way to argue with a man who always knew better than anyone else.

"It was only when I went to college that I discovered I had an identity." She was saying nothing new. We both knew well the brutality of the games her father had played on her. "I switched majors in the middle of my first semester without telling him. Then I met you."

"You don't need to tell me this," I pleaded. "Get to the point. I have to find you!"

But she went on, detailing the way her father had cut her off, the threats he'd made when we got married, then the lull in the storm, as if Jim Barker had decided to let her outgrow it.

"One day, I got a call from his executive secretary." Cleveland, I thought. Jim Barker's headquarters. "She'd seen the way my dad was isolating himself from me, and she offered to try to mend the fences, at least to give me news. After awhile, she'd call from home just to say 'hi.' We became friends. This was about a year ago. Later, Dad started phoning me, but only to ask me to come back and take over, never to tell me what was happening. Ellen did that" — Ellen must have been the secretary's name — "and she'd take letters from me and my mom."

Karen turned her head to hear something from somebody off camera, and then she said, "Fifteen minutes." She faced me again. "I have to hurry this, Ben. Back when I left college and married you, I still didn't have my identity together. You told me that, when you looked in my eyes, you couldn't see anything — just black holes."

I leaned closer. Her eyes. Something about —

"I went down to the church around the corner one Sunday morning when you were on the job somewhere. Took the kids too. It scared me to death, but the people there were so friendly and alive that I went back."

"And you met God," I murmured, looking at her eyes, seeing something there.

She went on. "I never knew what it was, why there was such an emptiness to everything I thought and did. No matter how hard I've tried, my life has always been in two dimensions. You know that, Ben. You've seen it."

"I know," I said, remembering the times I'd lain in bed wondering if I'd ever know the stranger beside me.

"When I started going to church, I realized that the third dimension must be God. I'd been trying to find my identity in myself, but I didn't have any resources to do anything but hate Dad and be hurt by him and want him to love me."

She looked pathetic for a moment, vulnerable. Then she spoke again. "I found out that Jesus could offer me forgiveness for my anger and bitterness. He could give me a new life."

I knew it was important to her, but I needed even more to know where she was, who had taken her.

"Get on with it, Karen." But I knew I wouldn't fast forward. I was fascinated by her eyes. How long was it since I'd been home — three weeks? Two jobs back-to-back with a one-day stopover in Mexico City. How could she change so much in three weeks?

"So I gave him my life, what there was of it. And then I phoned Dad, because he had to know. Ellen couldn't get him to pick up the phone until I explained it to her and she convinced him it was a crisis. Finally he came on the line and I told him."

"Why, Karen?"

"You've got to understand, Ben. He's made me into his little slave all my life, and now I've found out that everything I had was meaningless. I've got a relationship with God, and I know who I am. He had to hear it. One thing, though — I was surprised at how scattered he seemed, as if he couldn't quite take it in. He sounded old."

While I was having trouble understanding her faith, I was clear about the danger she'd put herself in. Jim Barker lived for control. "Two days later, his secretary called me and said Dad was in touch with some kind of deprogrammer. Are there still people like that around? Dad said he'd had enough, and I was coming into the business whether I wanted to or not. I'd been brainwashed by the university and by you, and now some cult had taken over my life.

"There's not much time now. Ellen says Dad's going to send someone with a letter asking me to leave you and take over the business. If I agree to go quietly, they'll bring in a moving van and clean out the house. I'm supposed to write you a Dear John letter. Dad will take care of the kids for the month I'm with the deprogrammer. The alternative is that he'll smear your reputation, get you fired, and make sure we are ruined financially. He's got the power.

"I've decided to try to beat him to it and

clear out before his men get here. Jeff is supposed to watch for you and tell you where I've gone, but he has to make some arrangements in Canada in case I don't get away on my own. He's going tonight — that's Sunday. You're not due back for awhile, so hopefully it'll all work out. I'm leaving tomorrow afternoon when Jeff gets back."

Sunday night. I'd come back Monday, and she was gone. Barker's goons had arrived Monday morning and Jeff had missed the whole thing. Great.

"Ben, I love you. Things haven't been fantastic for us lately. You've been away so much and I've been so messed up. But we'll be together again." She looked off camera again. "I'm almost out of time, but I have one more thing to ask. If Dad's people come for me before I can get away, I'm going to go with them, and I want you to stay away. I know what I believe, and no deprogrammer is going to shake me from it. My dad will see the light, and he'll have to let me go. But if you come looking for me, he's going to hurt you, Ben. Ellen says he still blames you for most of my rebellion against him. So don't come after us. Please, Ben."

The screen went blank, and I stared at it until the buzzing static crept into my consciousness. I clicked off the set and watched

90

the wallpaper until I heard a knock at the door.

"Ben?"

"Yeah."

Jeff came in, looking awkward. "I wanted to tell you that I'm sorry for the whole kidnapping thing. Karen's idea. The afternoon before you came home I went to Canada to help Dave get the cabin set up and Killer moved over. We weren't sure we'd need it, but if Karen did get snatched before she could move out, she wanted me to get you out of the way. I misjudged how fast they'd move. By Monday noon the place was empty."

"So you waited for me to come home."

"I live across the street. You wouldn't know that because you're only home a few days a month. When you pulled up, I phoned Dave to leave the car at McDonald's, and then I kidnapped you."

"Meanwhile Karen's getting her mind scrambled by some brainwasher. Do you know where she is?"

"No. Probably somewhere close. There would be no end of trouble getting Karen and two kids to Cleveland without anyone suspecting."

"So what would it be — a rented house? A motel?"

"I would guess a house. I suspect Barker's hired someone who's a big champion of civil liberties and knows just what keys to turn to talk people out of their faith."

I got up and stared out the window. The rain was starting again, sliding between the bare branches of a gnarled fruit tree in the back yard. "I thought deprogramming was something that died in the seventies."

"Not if you've got the money to hire some wacko with the right talents. There are still lots of crusaders out there. He just had to find one that was down on his luck."

"Can she resist him?"

"I don't know."

I looked at him intently for a few seconds. "You know what I'm going to do."

"Yes."

"Will you help me?"

"Karen wanted you to stay away."

"The guy's messing with my wife's head."

"If you try to get her, he'll kill you. We've got the evidence that he means business."

"Not if I kill him first."

"You're not thinking, Ben."

"It's not something I have to think about. Are you going to help me or not?"

He stared at the floor and scuffed his foot along a baseboard. When he looked up, I knew what the answer would be. "Okay, but we have to work together. No heroics from you. If I get killed, it'll be a long time before I forgive you. And I won't be involved in killing anyone."

"So where do we start?"

"That's easy," Jeff said. "I'm flying to Cleveland."

"Ellen, the secretary."

"Ellen."

"Why not phone her?"

"She's really spooked. Karen tried to call her before the snatch, and she hung up on her."

"I should be the one going."

"You'd be recognized. Besides, it was your car that crossed the border and you're the one who lied to the official. If you tried to cross back, you might be identified from the missing person report."

I sat down on the edge of the bed. "What am I supposed to do in the meantime?"

With a trace of humor, he said, "Lie low and get some rest. People out there don't seem to like you."

EIGHT

"You have to understand about Jeff," Dave said. We were sitting in the kitchen over a late breakfast, Dave, Edith, and I. Earlier that morning, he had driven his brother to the Vancouver airport for a 7:00 A.M. flight to Toronto and Cleveland. Jeff had insisted on paying for it himself. I, of course, got left behind. Good old Ben Sylvester was still in hiding.

"What do I need to understand?" I asked, pretending ignorance, remembering the moments when Jeff had teetered on the edge of sanity or had gone too far with the pistol-whipping.

"We came from an abusive home. For some reason, Jeff got the worst of it, but he coped by retreating into himself."

"The resistance to pain," I murmured.

"Pardon me?"

"He told me that people who threatened him with pain only made him angry, not afraid."

"He's too angry. In fact, he just plain scares me," Edith said carefully. "I've seen it on the street. Always scares me."

I looked puzzled. "We used to be street workers with addicts, drunks, the homeless," Dave put in.

"You two?"

"We don't look the part, do we," Edith said. "Just like Jeff doesn't look like a librarian. Looks more like a soldier of fortune."

"So is Jeff all right, going to Cleveland to talk a reluctant secretary into spilling hush-hush information?"

"I think so," Dave said. "He's not a psychotic. A lot of things changed for him when he met Christ. You've got to recognize that his anger when he was tortured was a reaction from his past. Since he came back, he's been trying to deal with the mix of emotions that his experience created. We're praying the Lord will heal him."

I shifted uncomfortably. Edith noticed and tried to give me a reassuring look. "You don't have to embrace our faith, Ben. We are who we are, so we talk about it. But we won't stop feeding you if you choose your own path."

"I hope not," I said. "I tend to enjoy a meal or two just about every day." Outside rain was falling steadily, and it seemed to surround the sense of peace I felt there in that kitchen, talking to Dave and Edith. I could hardly be blamed for failing to understand them, never having been particularly religious myself, but it seemed they'd found a corner on safety and confidence. They were certainly taking care of me. On the way back from the airport, Dave had bought me some clothes at a thrift store and shaving gear at a pharmacy.

Dave sipped thoughtfully on his coffee. "I helped Karen make the video. The church has a camera. The one thing she wanted me to make sure you understood was the change in her since she met Christ."

"You make it sound like I won't even know her anymore."

"Maybe you won't. She's changed to an amazing degree, as if she's ready to embrace life for the first time."

"When did you meet her?"

"A couple of months ago. We took a week off to visit Jeff. Actually, Jeff hardly knew her, but I noticed your family. One of your boys was acting up, so I stopped to clown with him a bit and get him out of the mood. Karen and Edith started talking. It seemed to us that Karen was really searching."

"For what?" I asked, though I didn't want to hear the answer. The atmosphere was getting too thick for me.

"Meaning, I guess. Answers. Maybe she didn't even know herself. But we recognize a search for God when we see it."

"How could you read God into the situation? You'd only just met her."

"Because she was attending a church even though she didn't know anyone there. Because she was talking about needing direction."

"Look, Dave," I said slowly. "I've been married to Karen for seven years, and you met her two months ago. That makes me very suspicious that you may not have had as clear a perception of her as I do."

Edith put her hand on my arm. "Ben, you've got to understand that the Karen you're searching for is not the Karen you're going to find. In the last six months or so, you've lost track of her."

"I can't accept that."

"Did you know she was searching for God? Did you see how important the church was to her?"

"Sort of. I thought it was a phase."

"It's not entirely your fault," she said. "Karen was worried you'd try to stop her if she got too serious."

"Why would I do that?"

"Because you don't want to share her with anyone," Dave put in, "even a crucified and resurrected Messiah."

I stared at him, trying not to show that he'd struck a nerve. After some small talk, I made an excuse and went to my bedroom. They didn't understand. How could they know how close I'd come to discovering Karen's soul, hidden by all the defenses she'd created? No one knew her like I did. How could she have changed radically without me knowing it? I'd only been gone three weeks.

But Karen was used to hiding things. It was well within her power to make a commitment to her faith and then not tell me. She was insecure. She didn't know who she was, even now.

The old chestnut has it that absence makes the heart grow fonder. But while the rain turned the world outside to shades of gray, I wondered if I'd lost her after all. Maybe absence gave the heart time to find another allegiance. I wondered if my secret fear all along had been that she'd finally discover herself and wouldn't need me any more.

I'm sure on a sunny day, in a situation when I wasn't a prisoner, Dave and Edith's conversation wouldn't have gotten to me. Of one thing I was certain — I never would have stopped Karen from chasing after her faith. There was no doubt about that. But I felt a chill in my heart just the same.

The next few days weighed heavily. Dave, I noticed, kept his blue Honda in his garage and only drove it after dark. I didn't go out at all. For someone who had to be in control of his life, I was learning a whole new discipline, one I rapidly came to loathe. Dependence didn't wear well on me.

Several times I replayed Karen's video, watching her eyes. Even then I was beginning to realize that the masks were gone, that I could see deeper into her soul than I ever had when we interacted face-to-face. Edith's words hovered in my memory — "The Karen you're searching for is not the Karen you're going to find" — until I thought I would go crazy with the sound of them.

Clearly Dave and Edith saw me as hostile and possessive, but it was only my way of getting around in a world that doesn't shift unless it gets pushed. The strong inherit the earth. The wimps get to be the victims. I refused to be a wimp.

That night I had a dream in which Hans, now fully back in action, went to the police and described a blue Honda that forced him off the road. The police traced the license number and came knocking on Dave's door.

In my dream, the two cops were nine feet tall and Dave, being so much smaller and a decent, honest man to boot, led them right to me. They hauled me screaming to a cell in the bowels of the police station, where I was left to rot.

Near morning, the dream switched to Karen, sitting in a small room with a crazed man who kept shouting at her, "Recant! Recant!" My kids were watching at the window, their faces in shadow so that I could not see their expressions or read their emotions. I tried to break the door down, but it was solid steel, and Karen kept looking at me and mouthing the word, "No."

I woke speaking her name, the pillow wet. Angry, I got up and washed my face in the bathroom down the hall. Unless I could soon bring some control into the situation, I feared I would keep on having these dreams until they drove me insane.

For one wild moment, as I stared at my stubbled face in the mirror, I imagined myself walking boldly out of the house, letting Hans find me, then turning the tables on him so he'd have to tell me where Karen was. It was nonsense, of course. Hans was too deadly a foe. I didn't even have a penknife, let alone the kind of weapon that would give me the upper hand.

There was a knock on the bathroom door, and Dave said, "Are you all right, Ben?" I realized then I'd left the sink tap on, the water gushing through the overflow hole.

"Yeah, I'm fine," I said, turning off the tap and opening the door.

"You're probably getting stir crazy." He was dressed in his customary sweater and tie, ready to go off to the church to do whatever preachers do during the week. "Jeff will be back tomorrow. He phoned a few minutes ago."

"Did he get the information?"

"Yes."

"Well?"

"He wouldn't tell me on the phone. He doesn't want you to act without him."

"He's scared."

"Of what?"

"Of what Karen will think of him. She doesn't want me to rescue her, believes her father will hurt me. If Jeff lets me go off on my own and I get maimed, he's got to answer to Karen." It didn't matter. The only important thing was that he had the information we needed to find my wife.

But I was surprised at Dave's plan. Touching my arm, he said, "Get dressed. We're going for a drive."

"Why?"

"We have to talk."

"I thought I was lying low."

"It's early. You can wear a hat, and we can head out of town where no one's likely to spot us."

"Are you going to lay some religious trip on me?"

"Maybe. We'll see."

I ate breakfast quickly, not because I was looking forward to the talk, but because I was eager to get out anywhere, for any reason. Dave made me wear an old hat and an overcoat. We sped out of town faster than I expected a preacher to drive, picking up the Dewdney Trunk Road and heading toward Maple Ridge. Once we were well underway, Dave started his spiel.

"I wanted to tell you about the things I believe. It's important."

"There's no point to this," I protested. "You're going to reel off some mumbo-jumbo and I'm not interested."

"Who said anything about making you interested? Your wife has embraced a faith that's changed her profoundly. I want you to understand what's happened to her. If you don't buy it, that's your right. But shut up and listen for awhile."

I listened. What he told me had epic overtones, the story of mankind from paradise to destruction to new hope. This guy actually believed in absolute good and evil, in a God who made and planned everything, then sent his Son to rescue us when we went off the rails. He even used the word *sin* without a snicker.

Finally I'd had enough. "Where do you live, Dave? We're at the end of the twentieth century and you're talking dark ages. Do you honestly believe that all our achievements are corrupted, that everybody on earth is doomed without Jesus?"

We had reached Maple Ridge, a moderately sized city, and Dave headed north toward twin snow peaks. "Golden Ears," he murmured. "See the way the peaks look like animal ears? There's a provincial park up there." I found out later he'd even got that wrong. The park was named after the eyries of golden eagles.

"Stop trying to buy time, Dave. Why are you laying all this religion on me and what makes you think I don't understand Karen anymore? She's my wife. Unless someone's been doing mind control on her, I know her better than you do."

We began to wind upward into the forest. I felt like he was taking me to Never-Never Land, and I hoped Captain Hook or Tinkerbell weren't waiting around the next bend. Dave's religion was too bizarre to connect it with life as I knew it.

"Karen was brutalized mentally and emotionally by her father," Dave went on. "It left her with hardly any identity of her own."

"Tell me something new."

"In the last little while, she's started to find out who she is, or who God intended her to be."

"And?"

"And she was confused by what she saw."

"Why?"

"You tell me," he said. "I'd really like you to explain to me who you think she is."

"She's a giving and capable person. Always does the right thing in the right way. But you just have to look at her sideways and her confidence evaporates. So what confused her about her new identity?"

"Anger. If you can imagine someone who has been held in slavery and is suddenly free, you can be sure that she's going to have ambivalent feelings toward her former captor even if he is her father. But it goes deeper. She's learning to be a person and not to be walked on by everyone who takes advantage of her. But she's frightened of her potential to be aggressive. It's even worse when she remembers that she's got the potential as well to choose Christ's way or use her freedom as an excuse for sin." We pulled into a parking lot at the end of the road, mountains all around us, a river running hard just below the car.

"She's a forgiven sinner, Ben, and she's working through all of what that means, plus she's trying to deal with the anger over her past in contrast to the new life she's living as a follower of Christ." He saw puzzlement in my eyes. "She's like a prisoner who's been freed and has to balance the joy of freedom with the anguish of her past. You need to grasp that she's on the way to healing, but she needs love and support along the way."

"I don't understand your religion," I said. "You sound like some kind of propaganda machine."

"You probably understand more than you think. I'll bet you could recite back to me most of what I've told you."

"Why should I even try?"

"So I won't think you're unintelligent."

I snorted. "Okay, you claim human beings are all wrong. We've rebelled against God and brought judgment on ourselves."

"So far so good."

"Then along came Jesus. You say he's the Son of God and died to take the punishment God was going to dump on us. Then he rose from the dead. Am I still on track?"

"More or less. Your account's a bit sparse."

"And you say that Karen's pledged some sort of undying allegiance to Jesus, and he's transformed her."

"Yes. You'll notice the difference when you see her."

"And I'm the tooth fairy."

"Pardon me?" Canadian politeness.

I glared at him, angry at being told tall tales. "Or maybe you're Peter Pan and just need to grow up. Look, Dave, this stuff doesn't wash. I appreciate you explaining what Karen's into, but to me it's nothing more than any other wacko story about good conquering evil. If you want a convert, choose someone whose elevator doesn't go to the top floor. Mine does."

He contemplated that for a few seconds, then started the car. "Think about one thing, Ben. If we human beings are not a fallen race, then why are we such miserable failures at being human beings?"

He drove me home. All the way, I thought about the question, but for the life of me I couldn't think of an answer.

NINE

Jeff flew in the next afternoon. While Dave went to get him at the airport, I waited, my stomach in knots, a sense of doom hovering at the edge of my consciousness.

Jeff was tired when he arrived, his face white and haggard. But there was a light of triumph in his eyes that compelled him to reject Edith's offer of supper so that we could gather in the living room and talk.

"Her name's Ellen Dunsmore. For an executive secretary in a posh situation, that woman was scared. I phoned her at work and she hung up on me. When I called her at home, she told me to leave her alone."

"You called her back?" I asked.

"Four more times. She hung up each time. Then on the fifth try, I asked her if she cared more about her job than Karen's safety. She listened and I told her all I knew."

"What did she tell you?" Dave asked, trying to get it out of Jeff faster.

"She kept me cooling my heels for four and a half days. Said she needed to find out more and to think about how much she was going to reveal. I did a lot of sightseeing."

"Come on, Jeff," I urged.

"Karen's about two hundred and fifty miles from here. In Canada."

"How did they get her across the border?"

"Private plane. They passed her off as a secretary. She went voluntarily."

"The kids?"

"On vacation somewhere in Arizona with Karen's parents."

"Why did she go along with all this?"

"Barker's still got a lot of power over her. She was afraid for your safety, and Barker has her kids."

"So what are they doing to her?"

"Barker hired some guy who's an expert at talking people out of their beliefs."

"A deprogrammer."

"The sophisticated variety. Apparently he's using everything from hypnosis to drugs. Sorry, Ben."

"I want her out of there," I said, my voice cracking.

"We'll do it. But first we have to put the pieces together. The way I figure it, Barker hired Hans to do you in. Ellen didn't know anything about Hans, but I'm guessing Barker wanted you dead while the deprogrammer worked on Karen. Then Barker would tell her you died in an accident, and that would be enough to tip her back into her daddy's arms."

"The man must be crazy if that's the way it is."

"You have no idea, Ben, how much he blames you for destroying his dream of Karen taking over his company. He thinks you poisoned her mind and drove her into her religion. As far as he's concerned, he's saving his daughter from disaster. Ellen Dunsmore went into great detail."

"Where's Karen?"

"Electar."

I'd completely forgotten about the town Jim Barker had founded and the strange name he'd given it — some English derivative of the Greek word for amber and the source of our word *electricity*. Electar was a Barker experiment, a resort village on the west side of Okanagan Lake. The workers produced small electronic components in a setting where all their needs were provided for. While they made barely adequate wages, they were supplied with housing, food, a school, a pool of vehicles, and as much recreational opportunity as anyone could ever want.

People had told Barker the plan was too science fiction and not economical since costs were lower in the States. But he had some wild dream of being father of yet another high-tech revolution that would change society as we know it. As far as I was concerned, it sounded too much like the failed communist dream to ever have a hope of succeeding.

"So how do we get into Electar, and where exactly are they holding Karen?" I asked.

"Ellen said the best way in is by canoe at night. There's a dock on Okanagan Lake just below Electar. She gave me a map to show which building Karen's in."

The warning that had been droning around me suddenly grew louder. Something was wrong here. Something about Ellen Dunsmore was wrong. And Jim Barker was coming off too Machiavellian, even for him. I could picture him hiring a deprogrammer to talk Karen out of her religion, but I couldn't see him sanctioning drugs.

"Jeff," I said, "go over Ellen Dunsmore's story again. How did she first contact Karen? What's her involvement?"

"Why?"

"Just indulge me."

"Seems like all I do is indulge you. Well . . . okay. Ellen started by acting as an intermediary for Karen's mother. Karen would write to Ellen's address and Ellen would get the letters to her mom."

I'd always found it hard to maintain a clear image of Mrs. Barker. She was a shadow, a gray lady living like a constant backdrop to her husband's powerful assertiveness. Not that she wasn't nice or pleasant or even good humored. But she never challenged Jim Barker in any way, and he always had the floor. God only knew what she had been through.

But for now I was more concerned about Ellen Dunsmore. Jeff went on. "She called Karen a few times to relay messages, and they became friends. Ellen obviously felt sorry for Karen and her mom."

"Wasn't she taking a risk?"

"She told me it was worth it. A lot of the things Barker is into have made her feel dirty. Helping Karen was a way of cleansing herself."

"So why did she stay in her job if she didn't believe in what Barker was doing?"

"I don't know. She was vague on that point."

"You asked her?"

"Sure. I wondered about it myself."

I got up and walked to the window, shading anyone's view of me with the half-drawn drape. Outside the rain had stopped, leaving behind the gray, like a paint wash in preparation for new colors that would have to come eventually.

"I've got to think about this, Jeff."

"What's to think about?"

I turned to look at him, sitting somewhat uneasily in an armchair, Dave and Edith on the sofa. All three had a quizzical look. "What if we're totally wrong about this? What if someone's pulling off a grand deception?"

"I thought you had your villain," Jeff muttered.

"Neither Karen nor I have had any real interaction with Jim Barker for years. He calls Karen regularly but only to lay a trip on her about the way she's supposedly wasting her life. He never says anything about himself. Karen's mom says he's getting old and tired. He forgets things."

"What's your point?" Dave asked.

"All our information is coming from Ellen Dunsmore. She's the one who warned Karen about Jim's plans. And she's the one who conveniently has a map of Electar and knows the precise building where Karen's being held. She even gave us a strategy to sneak into the town without being noticed."

"You're on the wrong track, Ben," Jeff said. "I talked to the woman, and she's on the level."

"I'm a political scientist, Jeff. I'm not trained to see the best in people. Sure, the simplest solution is to believe that Barker's finally gone off the deep end, but he's slipped pretty far, even for him, if he's kidnapped his own daughter and agreed to have her drugged, not to mention putting out a hit on his son-in-law. To top it off, Ellen is too convenient a helper."

"She cares about Karen."

"And yet she's continued to work for a man like Barker."

"Okay, Ben," Jeff said, picking it up. "Are you saying that Jim Barker didn't take Karen?"

"I'm saying Ellen Dunsmore isn't on the level. Maybe she's got some sort of leverage over Barker. Maybe she's doing things in his name."

"You've got no evidence for it."

"Suppose, Jeff, that Barker has become incompetent. Couldn't Ellen have engineered the snatch herself?"

"Why?"

"I don't know why."

Dave made as if he wanted to say something but thought better of it.

"Karen went voluntarily," Jeff continued. "I can't see that she would have done that without something definite from her dad —

a letter or a phone call."

"She might have gone with someone if Ellen herself gave the authorization. She trusted Ellen."

"Meanwhile you don't trust anyone," Edith said suddenly. "First you thought Jeff was a kidnapper, then Jim Barker, and now all of a sudden this Ellen is a prime suspect."

"You can hardly blame me, Edith. This hasn't exactly been a picnic."

"I think we should just bring the police in and let them handle it," Dave said.

"We can't," I said icily, "because your really bright brother took us into Canada under false pretenses, and I'm officially a missing person. Besides, Electar's a company town. If the police show up, Karen will be hidden so well that none of us will find her."

A sudden thought alarmed me. "Jeff," I said, "did you give Ellen Dave's phone number?"

"Yes. She's supposed to contact us if she hears anything else."

"With a phone number you can trace an address."

"So?"

"So, if she's the one who hired Hans, he'll be able to track us down."

"Come on, Ben. This paranoid routine

doesn't wash. What's wrong with you?" But there was a hint of uncertainty in Jeff's voice.

"What's wrong with me is that I feel like a fly in a spider web. Your Ellen is too helpful. It's a trap."

"What would she gain from kidnapping Karen?"

"I already told you I don't know. Look, people, I'm feeling a little outnumbered here."

"She's your wife, Ben," Edith said. "It's your decision."

"Do you have a plan?" Dave asked.

"Not really. I just know I have to get to Electar."

"I'm going too," Jeff said.

"But I don't trust Ellen. We have to find another way in. We'll just have to figure it out when we get there."

"Need a third person?" Dave's tone didn't reveal much eagerness.

"You've got a wife to come home to. Three people will only clutter up the land-scape."

Dave's look of relieved disappointment was almost comical, but I wasn't laughing. Even though I had much more information now, it had turned the situation into a swamp where nothing looked like a sure path. Either Jim Barker or Ellen Dunsmore was the villain. Or Ellen was working for someone else still unknown to me. Or Ellen and Barker were in cahoots. This last one seemed less likely unless the scheme was far more complicated than I thought.

Our only option was to go to Electar as soon as possible. If Hans was on our trail again, we'd have to leave by the next morning. I doubted that his kill mandate would include Dave and Edith as long as Jeff and I were out of the way. Fortunately, Dave had added warm coats and waterproof boots to our thrift shop wardrobes, so we would not need outfitting.

"We'll have to rent a car," I said.

"Use mine," Dave offered.

"No thanks. If Hans is on to us, I don't want something he can recognize."

"I'll drive you to Abbotsford before dawn tomorrow. You can pick up a rental there."

"On my credit card, I suppose," Jeff said.

"Sorry." I gave him a half smile. "We can't afford to have my name traced. If it makes you feel any better, I'll reimburse you when this is over."

"If we're both corpses, it won't matter anyway," he said. Edith winced.

"Are you sure this is the only way?" Dave asked.

"No," I admitted. "This is a stupid idea, and I'm not ready for it. Jeff's crazy to go with me."

"So let's get some supper and make an early night of it," Jeff said. Clearly, this was the adventure of his life.

"Ben, would you mind if I talked to Jeff alone?" Dave said.

"Help me in the kitchen, Ben," Edith put in quickly. I had no choice. Even though I needed Jeff, I wasn't about to let him come if he could be talked out of it. They took about ten minutes, and then both of them came into the kitchen looking subdued. Dave sat down on a chair and stared at me searchingly.

"You expected me to try to stop you, didn't you, Ben," he said. "Want to know why I didn't?"

"Sure."

"Don't flatter yourself that you've got a good plan. It stinks, and the police should take care of it. But both of you are too stubborn to listen to me. I warned Jeff at the beginning of this not to get involved. If a kidnapping was being planned, there are trained people who can deal with it. We had no idea then how dangerous this was going to be, but I couldn't go along with the deception Jeff was going to have to pull on you."

"So why did you help him?"

"Because he would have done it anyway and probably ended up in jail unless I watched out for him." Jeff looked grieved.

"Sorry," Dave went on. "Jeff, you're big on bravado but not much on necessary caution. I helped you to protect you. Karen obviously feared for your safety, maybe even your life. As it turns out, she was right."

"Dave," I said, "this might look like musical chairs, but I need to talk to you too. Jeff, finish setting the table. I hate domestic chores."

Dave followed me into the living room. "This is awkward," I said. "Jeff's a strange guy. Unstable. Sometimes I think I can trust him, then he gets weird on me."

Dave went to the front window and stared out of the crack in the curtain. "Jeff lost a piece of himself when he took that job overseas and got tortured. It's like a kid I met once on the street. Someone had beaten him half to death a few months before, and even when his body recovered he couldn't look anyone in the eye. Any loud noise would send him up a wall. Jeff's not over his post-trauma. I think he figures rescuing Karen will give him back his manhood."

"So is he okay? I have to count on him, and I can't use a loose cannon."

"I think so." Dave didn't look terribly sure about it.

We went back and sat down to supper, but before I could pick up a roll to butter it, Dave's look stopped me. "Grace," I muttered to myself. It was like a scene from *Father Knows Best* living with these people. They bowed their heads and Dave prayed, not just for the food but for Jeff and me and the journey. He asked forgiveness for the deceptions and the violence against Hans and his boys, on and on. But instead of my usual irritation, I felt a glow at the concern of these good people, their baffling faith in someone they couldn't see.

Later, I took off my arm bandage. The sling had long gone. The wound didn't look too bad at all, though it still ached. The blade the guy had used on me had been extremely thin, so not much of the flesh had torn. With a borrowed pair of scissors and tweezers, I took out the stitches. Then, carefully, I began exercising the arm. The sooner I got it going again, the better.

I fell asleep with Dave's prayer echoing in my ears. "And bless Jeff and Ben, and keep them safe . . ." Despite his confidence in God, I had noticed him doing a second round to check the locks on the doors and windows.

TEN

The road seemed to climb forever. It crossed the snowline and then just kept going up, challenging our four-door Tercel, mocking our hope to find an end to it. The Coquahalla Highway was someone's dream to cut miles off the trip to the provincial interior by burning the life out of any vehicle greedy enough to take it on. Presumably the Ministry of Tourism had been outvoted by the car mechanics' lobby.

We'd had no trouble at the rental agency, but then, I was hardly paying attention to the transaction and would have missed the trouble if there was any. My whole attention since we'd left Mission had been on trying to spot anyone tailing us. Dave and Jeff had been kind, not saying a thing about the fact that neither Hans nor anyone else had come to break down the doors overnight. I reminded them, of course, that Ellen Dunsmore had provided us with her own foolproof plan to get to Karen. If she was masterminding a plot, her henchmen would be waiting for us on the dock at Electar.

It was an amazingly clear day, the snow on the mountain peaks giving them a sharp knife edge against the sky. Where the clouds had gone once we left the Fraser Valley, I did not know. Nor did I much care. But I did have to admit that the view was spectacular, all mountains and rocks and trees.

We came to a slow-down in the traffic flow, at least twenty cars ahead of us. Then the whole line stopped. "Avalanche control," Jeff muttered impatiently.

"So tell me, how do you control an avalanche?"

"You may have noticed round platforms at the side of the road," he answered, with nothing better to do. "They mount a gun on the platform and fire into the hillside to bring down the snow."

"Which buries the road."

"No, they do it regularly before enough snow can build up to make it a hazard. There's no risk of it reaching the highway."

"Which is why they won't let anyone drive on it until they're finished."

"Get a life, Ben," he retorted. I clammed up. Obviously he was right, because when we went on with our climb, there were no signs of bulldozers clearing the highway. Jeff drove fast, pushing the car hard. The road varied from four to six lanes, depending on whether or not the slowpokes needed a safe haven on particularly steep grades.

We came to a toll booth, and Jeff paid his ten bucks for the privilege of wrecking the car further. But mercifully, after a few more miles, we started to descend. We turned off at Merritt, a small town made significant by the highway, and stopped at a restaurant for lunch. I forget what I ate. My mind was otherwise occupied. They could have served me sheep brains and I wouldn't have noticed.

As we got into the car, Jeff grinned and said, "Now we get to go really high." He wasn't kidding. After half an hour of two-lane secondary road, a stretch that the previous provincial government had left undone to save money, we picked up the Okanagan Connector, a real bear of a climb to almost fifty-six hundred feet, just over a mile high. Considering that we had started out at virtually sea level, I marveled that the Tercel was still humming along.

This travelogue may not sound like much, but it was a stunning front to what was going on in the background — the hammering of my heart. I was nearly apoplectic with fear for Karen and fear for me. This was the stupidest idea anyone had ever had, and I'd put myself right in the middle of it. With any luck, we were walking into a trap, and the only faithful companion I had was some burned-out guy desperate to prove he was still a man.

But buried in the terror was a spark of crazy joy. For the first time since all this had started, I had a measure of control. I wasn't just a pawn to be jerked around at everyone else's whim. Whether or not we'd get Karen back, at least I was going to have a shot at saving her.

"Ben?" Jeff said as we reached the summit of the Connector and started the steep run down to Okanagan Lake.

"What?"

"Why do you never say anything about your kids?"

"You said they were safe. Karen's the one we're rescuing."

"Do you miss them?"

"Sure."

"How old are they?"

"Jack's six. Jimmie's four."

"Five."

"Excuse me?"

"Jimmie turned five two weeks ago while you were away. So what's the deal?"

"I'm away a lot."

"And you don't like kids."

"The Inquisition ended a few centuries

ago, Jeff." I stared out the side window, watching the snow get thinner as we descended. This guy was uncanny in his ability to rattle my cage.

What right did he have to question me about my kids? If I'd let him go on, he'd probably have told me I was afraid of them. It was nothing like that. Some people are kid people, some aren't.

If I'd been able to be home more, maybe I'd have connected with them better. I loved them. That was worth something. Wasn't I on my way to rescue them?

Too much introspection. I stared out the window as we went under the only wildlife overpass I'd ever seen. The highway, Jeff told me, had been built with numerous tunnels under it so that animals could continue their normal migration patterns. But here, the terrain had been too steep for a tunnel and so an expensive concrete overpass had been built. Of course, it would take an awfully brave bundle of walking venison to actually use the thing. Nothing moved on it as we went under.

"Must be nice to be a deer," Jeff said.

"Yeah, must be great to listen to blasting rifles and twanging bowstrings. How about that first twinge when a bullet or arrow hits you in the side?"

"The longer I know you, Ben, the more I appreciate your folksy humor. But you know what I really like about you?"

"What?"

"Not much."

"That makes two of us," I admitted. "Then why help me?"

"The thrill of the chase." Somehow I sensed he wasn't kidding.

"You're going to have to get serious about this. We're not playing war games."

"Oh, I'm serious all right."

"You're trying to recapture the man you thought you were before you did the dance of the burning cigarette in Thailand."

"Is that a question?"

"Observation."

"Why do you care why I'm helping you?"

"Because there will probably be some pain and terror before we're done. I don't even know how I'll perform, let alone you."

"Then let the cops handle it."

"They won't find Karen. We've got no evidence that anything criminal has even happened except for our being in the country under false pretenses. The cops would take a direct approach with these people, as in 'Are you holding a Karen Sylvester against her will?' 'Never heard of her, officer,' and that'd be the end of it."

"And you'd rather take control of the whole thing yourself."

There he went again — striking a nerve. So I didn't work well with other people. Was that such a big deal? Libertec was always on me about the same thing, but I got the job done. You bring in a committee and someone's bound to screw up.

As we came down the hill, a dark ribbon of lake emerged below, more like a wide river, though Jeff had told me Okanagan Lake was eighty miles long and incredibly deep. The vegetation grew sparse — scattered trees, mostly pines, separated by brown hillside. It was striking in a somber sort of way.

"Ten minutes to Kelowna," Jeff remarked.

"Clue me in on the geography again."

"Electar's on the west side of the lake. We pass a turnoff to it just up ahead. Kelowna's a city of something like a hundred thousand people. It's on the east side of the lake."

"Are we going to need water wings to cross?"

"Floating bridge," Jeff answered as the highway came out over a bluff and Kelowna opened up below us on the other side of the lake. Sure enough, there was a bridge lying right in the water, a gray ribbon leading to the city. I'd taken note of the turnoff to Electar a few miles back — two-lane paved road. Everything seemed so civilized it was hard to believe Karen might be a captive only a few miles away.

We planned to take a motel on the far end of Kelowna for the night, then head north about thirty miles to Vernon, the city at the north end of the lake. From there, we'd follow a road that wound along the west side of Okanagan Lake to Electar. Since Ellen was expecting us to come across the water by canoe, I'd convinced Jeff that the smartest move was to come down on Electar out of the hills.

As for locating Karen, all we had was Ellen's information. Maybe she had revealed the right building, maybe not. "And maybe she's on the level," Jeff told me angrily that night in the motel room. "Maybe your changes in the plan are going to get us both killed."

"I don't want to take a chance. We'll only get one shot at this, and I don't want to get picked off before I've had a good try at getting her out."

"Where do we hide the car?"

"I don't know."

"What supplies do you think we'll need?"

"Hard to say. Probably basic packs with

food to last us two or three days. At least we already have warm clothes." I'd noticed the night chill earlier. Kelowna was quite a bit higher than Mission, and the temperatures showed it.

"Guns?"

"Where are we going to get guns?"

"Knives then."

"Okay. Hunting knives."

Jeff looked relieved. Obviously this operation was beginning to wear on him. Sometimes he approached it like a little kid just about to dip into chocolate. But at other moments I saw tension in his face, a slight twitch in his left eye. This was make it or break it time for Jeff. I only wished I could guarantee his stability.

We studied a map of the area, picked up at a gas station, and discovered a road along the east side of the lake, north of Kelowna, that would bring us directly opposite Electar. If we could get high enough into the hills, we'd be able to look across the lake and see the layout of our destination through binoculars.

Jeff also pulled some sobering news out of a brochure. While the east side of the lake posed few dangers from wildlife, the west side was a good environment for rattlesnakes. High leather boots were advised, and we made plans to buy some as soon as the stores opened in the morning. At this rate, Jeff would soon reach the limit on his credit card.

Later, I lay awake listening to the splash of car tires from an evening shower. Crazy. Crazy. We had nothing set up, no strategy at all — just to blunder into Electar under cover of darkness and hope for the best. How many of the residents were enemies? Was Hans going to be waiting for us at the dock? Or had more thugs been hired so they could cover the whole town?

Karen. The struggle to know for sure what had happened to her was a gnawing pain that never went away. Probably I didn't want it to. I couldn't get rid of the premonition that this whole thing was far more dangerous than even Jeff and I feared.

Or maybe the scenario was completely different and we hadn't even met the real enemy yet. Whoever had sent Hans and his boys to kill us wasn't interested in playing cat and mouse. And the reason for the hit order had to be more than that Jim Barker hated me.

I'd been through too much. My body ached with muscle tension and my eyes burned. How much stress can a person take before the mythical snapping point is reached? Feeling as tired as I was, I wondered how many mistakes I might make when we reached Electar. Even one could be deadly.

Jeff, as usual, fell asleep right away. But he twitched often while I lay awake in the bed opposite his. A couple of times he muttered words I couldn't understand, and once he gave a little yell of fear. Probably he was rehearsing his performance over the next couple of days. It was as reassuring to me as having Jesse James offer to handle my financial affairs for free.

Eventually I fell asleep into my own nightmares, most of which ended badly. Jeff and I were as ready as we'd ever been, and the outcome could only be disastrous.

ELEVEN

Eleven A.M. The binoculars were as powerful as the over-eager sales clerk at the sports store had promised. We were on a ridge overlooking Okanagan Lake — Electar was a mile or so across, on the other side. We hadn't even needed to do any hiking. It turned out there was a viewpoint in Knox Mountain Park that gave us a perfect view. Across the lake were probably two hundred homes, including town-house clusters and some detached houses. The place was designed like a wheel with the streets running in concentric circles; five roads serving as spokes converged on a central open area with a large building at the center.

Jeff poked my arm to get possession of the binoculars. I'd been concentrating so hard that his interruption gave me a good chance to check out my startle response and find it working perfectly. No one could challenge the fact that we were pumped up. Both of us were distractible and clumsy, as if we were out of touch with our bodies, watching them from the outside, operating on remote control.

Across the narrow lake was Karen. Maybe.

And maybe Hans and his boys, if they'd survived the crash. And maybe death or dismemberment for Jeff and me. Facing it was like climbing forty flights of stairs — the farther we went, the harder it was to deal with the next part. By the time we got into the hills above Electar and came down in the darkness, we might have no resources left. Would one of us decide at the last minute to call it off?

I glanced at Jeff. He looked terrible, his face pale, almost gray, the skin creased with tension. I had my commitment to my wife to keep me going. What did he have except his wounded ego? His faith? Both were unknown quantities as far as I was concerned.

"What kind of security do you think they have?" Jeff asked.

"Search me. It's probably a controlled community, but there aren't any walls around it."

"Guards? Dogs?"

"I don't know."

"How can we find out?"

"Later. Let's try to spot the building where Ellen said Karen's being held."

"She might not be there." Jeff handed me the binoculars.

"It's all we've got," I muttered. With the binoculars I swept the little settlement, looking for the detached house, fourth from the end of the southern spoke road. I found it easily, taking mental note that it seemed to be the only one on the street with a high hedge or fence around it.

"If they're holding Karen," I said, "I wonder how many other people in the town are in on it. Are we facing a totally hostile crowd or just a few carefully chosen enemies?"

"It depends on how much of a hold they have on her. She went voluntarily. Maybe she's not much of a threat to them."

"But we're a threat. If Ellen's involved in this, Hans will be waiting for us on the dock." I used the binoculars to scan the waterfront area. There was a sizable dock and a marina next to it — maybe fifty pleasure craft. But I could see no one around. The boats were battened down for the winter.

"You're wrong about Ellen," Jeff told me again. "I think you're nuts to throw away her plan."

"Maybe I'm not," I said, making it clear from my tone that I wasn't prepared to discuss it. Surveying the town again, I tried to memorize the details as well as possible, including the large factory building on a ridge just above it and the school next to the factory. Quite an operation, I thought, giving grudging admiration to Jim Barker. Then my sweep went left and right to the approaches to Electar.

"We'll have to dump the car somewhere," I said. "Any ideas?"

"There's a provincial campground nearby."

"Probably closed."

"How about leaving the car at the side of the road with the hood up?"

"The only place to go for help is Electar. If their security people spot the car, they'll wonder why the driver didn't make an appearance in their fair town."

"Well, I'm sure not prepared to walk ten miles," Jeff told me.

"There must be logging roads up there. Surely we can hide a car for a day or two." I scanned until I spotted two logging roads, about a mile apart, running up into the hills. "We'll have to chance it."

"This is getting risky. The cloud cover's pretty heavy, and walking out of there in the dark won't be a piece of cake."

"We'll dump the car about four and start walking as soon as dusk hits."

Jeff thought for a moment, probably picturing our approach to Electar. "Does everybody know everybody else in that town? There couldn't be more than about five hundred people there."

"I don't know." Even as I said it, I saw how crucial the answer could be. If we would be spotted easily as strangers, we wouldn't have a prayer. I didn't fancy skulking through back yards to escape observation.

"Let's go," I said.

"Where?"

"To get some answers." We drove to the local Chamber of Commerce office. Outside I told Jeff, "Just go along with me and keep your mouth shut."

I walked in, pretending confidence. Jeff stood behind me, uncertain. A woman sat at the desk, smiling professionally.

"I'm serving as an agent for several fast-food franchise-oriented companies," I said. "We're checking out the potential in this area."

She frowned slightly, her eyes tinged with a hint of disbelief. "You didn't know that Kelowna is saturated with restaurants?"

"Not Kelowna as such," I said, backtracking quickly. "These are lower echelon companies that like to locate in smaller areas — Westbank maybe, or that company town across the lake . . ." I hesitated.

"Electar?" she said.

"Yes."

"Westbank might have some minimal potential. Electar's out."

"Why's that?"

"It's a planned community. They create all their own amenities. No chains."

"Who could I talk to over there?" I persisted. "Or is it one of those places with armed guards and dogs?"

"No, nothing like that. Electar's fairly self-contained, but it tries to relate to neighboring communities."

"In what ways?"

"They give tours. Their recreation center and pool are open to the public every evening."

I tried to shade the light that had gone on in my head. "Isn't Electar supposed to be a closed environment for the factory workers?"

"Nothing can be totally closed these days," she said. "Their recreation facilities are far bigger than they need. Letting others use them generates a lot of goodwill and keeps the residents from feeling too claustrophobic."

"No franchises?"

"Not a chance." She smiled. "Let me give you some numbers to call in Westbank." I dutifully took the slip of paper she passed me.

Outside in the car we worked on strategy.

There was no need to park miles away and walk in. We'd drive right into Electar as if wanting to use the pool. That would give us two or three hours to search for Karen before the recreation center closed.

Once again I had confirmation that Ellen was working for the opposition. If she had enough inside knowledge to be aware that Electar's dock was unguarded, she also knew there was a far easier way to get into the town. Why had she told us to sneak in by canoe when we could swim in Electar's pool any evening we wanted to?

But how many people were looking for us? Had Electar's security people been alerted? Maybe everyone in the town had been shown a photo of us, or at least had been given descriptions. We had no idea what sort of resistance we were facing. It was like walking into a lions' den without doing a lion census first. *Stupid* was the word I'd use.

I was angry that someone like Ellen would organize an ambush for us, and that she'd betrayed Karen with false friendship. What did she want that was worth tearing people's hearts out . . . or killing them? And where did Barker fit into this? Was she working for him? Did Barker really hate me enough to put out a hit on me?

But the one really nagging doubt was whether or not Karen was there. This could be Ellen's — or Barker's — last cruel joke. My fear was leading my mind to play three or four scenarios, all of them horrifying.

One: Karen wasn't in Electar, but Hans was waiting for us at the target house. Two: Karen had been there but they'd killed her, and now they were waiting for us. Three: Karen was there, but she was bait in a trap, and she'd have the privilege of watching me die. Four: Jeff and I would get past the opposition, find Karen, and not be able to get out of Electar before our enemies grabbed us.

That kind of thinking was nonproductive, but I couldn't get past it. I looked at Jeff as we sat in the car in the parking lot near the Chamber of Commerce. Could either of us come up with any kind of intelligent strategy? I could sense the fear rising in him, clouding his mind. What scenarios was Jeff playing?

"I don't see why we need a fancy plan," Jeff said finally. "Without knowing the layout, we're going to have to wing it anyway."

"And I suppose we've worked so well together in the past that we can read each other's minds," I said. "Look, if you want to go with me, we're going to spend the next few hours working on strategies."

"What about lunch?"

"Fast food," I told him. After a quick meal, we talked through our operation over and over, anticipating every conceivable possibility and deciding on reactions. Our only weapons would be our concealed knives, so we had to be prepared to major on wits. The hours passed, and we rehearsed everything until Jeff finally threw up his hands and refused to do any more.

Time was getting short, and neither of us was keen on supper. We had a light meal just to keep up our strength. I remembered a tough construction job I'd had between college years. Every morning I'd ridden twenty minutes to the job site. Instead of enjoying the trip, I'd reminded myself constantly that every minute that passed was one more step toward the moment when the agony of the day would begin.

I felt like that again. The jump from peace and freedom to terrifying risk was a short one. Soon — inevitably — we'd be in the soup. Before the night was out, there was a good chance I'd be dead and Jeff with me.

About 6:00, we drove north to Vernon and then headed south down the other side of the lake. Swimming started at 7:30, and we wanted to increase our chances by coming from an unexpected direction. Jeff drove and I sat staring, feeling disembodied again, savoring the passing moments before we made a leap into the dark.

Then with Electar no more than five miles away, Jeff, for no reason that I could see, pulled over.

"What are you doing?" I said, my voice showing an edge.

"You want me along?"

"Sure."

"What are you paying me?"

I stared at him. "Nothing. You know that."

"I'll go on one condition."

"What?"

"We're going to pray."

"Are you crazy?" I'd never been sure about this guy, and now the old doubts came rushing back.

"You don't have to do anything. Just listen." This twist was too bizarre for me. It was as if my emotions were being pushed off a cliff. I listened numbly.

"Lord, I know I'm ready for anything. Ben here isn't . . ." He paused and decided not to pursue it. "I know my motives are right. At least, I hope they are. All we want is Karen and the kids back safe with Ben. You know I've been trying to prove myself, but now that's not important — I'm not brave enough in myself to do this."

I was seething. Come on, come on. In another context it would have been embarrassing, but now it was just frustrating beyond belief. He went on, calling for God's strength and safety and success and who knows what else. I was used to recited prayers from childhood, but this was like an earnest conversation with someone in the back seat. Finally, he ended it and started the car. I stared out the window to hide my emotions.

The last few miles vanished like a breath. We reached Electar and headed down the northern spoke toward the rec center in the middle of the town. Then we were there, the center large and modern, ringed by parking lots.

A half mile south was Karen — maybe. Or maybe something else. There were no more minutes left, and the fear was so strong that I wanted to do nothing but go back to the motel and pull the covers over my head.

I looked at Jeff. He'd told his God that he was ready and I wasn't. From what I could see, neither of us had a chance this side of the grave.

TWELVE

There was no way to approach the house secretly — we saw that the moment we set out. Electar was organized for safety, and a burglar would not have had a chance in its streets. Every ten yards was a powerful street lamp. Each home had floodlights. It was like walking down the middle of a shopping mall.

We went immediately to Plan B. Instead of trying not to be seen, we walked casually down the sidewalks, keeping up a running conversation about hockey standings. The risk was that someone would spot us as strangers and call security. But no alarms were raised, though our discussion was stilted and unnatural.

Walking past the sedate, brightly lit townhouses, then single homes, I found it hard to believe we'd entered a potential war zone. The memory of Hans and his goons was losing its edge, and it seemed like all we needed to do was to walk up to the front door and ask, "Is Karen here?" The way we were going, we might have to do just that.

Only when we knew for sure what kind of fence was around the house would we know whether or not a strategy was possible.

We walked past it, still talking. The fence went more than three-quarters of the way around the house, with a high hedge across the front. There was a gate in the seven foot high fence on the left side, facing the street. From the street, the house was invisible.

As we walked, I casually threw a piece of meat over the fence, glad to be rid of it after it had smelled up my pocket since supper. There were no dog sounds from the other side — a mercy if we were planning to go over the fence.

Now that we had passed the house, it was hard to know what to do for an encore. I thought about it as we continued to walk and talk. The layout was basic. With all those lights, jumping the fence would bring too much risk. But the hedge had real possibilities. It wasn't solid.

I explained my plan to Jeff, who didn't think much of it. I didn't either. The best we could hope for was to stay out of sight long enough to get a good look at the house itself. From that point, the options were uncertain. All of our earlier planning looked pretty futile when we saw the actual situation.

We walked back, still talking. As we neared the house, I swept my gaze in as full a circle as possible, looking for other people on the street or peering out of windows. There was no sign of life, no cars approaching from either direction.

We pushed into the hedge, shoving ourselves in among the prickly branches until we could see the house but were invisible from the street. I held my breath, but there were no shouts, no shots, not even a "Come out with your hands up."

The house was not fancy — about fifty feet wide, with a large window to the left, then a door and two smaller windows on the right. The curtains were drawn. All the lights were on. There was no outside guard that we could see.

"What now?" Jeff whispered.

"We get closer," I told him. The fence and hedge, intended to hide the house from curious eyes, had created one disadvantage for the occupants — once someone was inside the perimeter, no one could see him from the street.

We ran across to the right corner of the house, cringing at the intensity of the floodlights on the lawn. Anyone looking out of a window could not help but notice us. I listened but heard nothing, so we moved down the side, which had only one glazed window. Bathroom. No sounds anywhere. In the back, there was a large sundeck. The fence continued right around the perimeter of the lot. At the far end of the house was a larger window. Probably that end contained the living room, dining room, and kitchen.

Carefully I climbed up on the sundeck, going over the railing and shuddering as my foot grated on the rough floor. I'd spotted a narrow gap in the kitchen curtain. Inching slowly over, I put my eye up to it. Inside, sitting at a small table, was a woman about thirty-five, dark hair, not Karen.

I motioned for Jeff to come up, which he did reluctantly, clumsily. With the noise he made, I was sure we'd be spotted, but the woman kept on reading her magazine. Jeff took a look and whispered hoarsely, "Ellen." Amazed, I stared at him, and he nodded to confirm what he had just said. This was Ellen Dunsmore, who was supposed to be in Cleveland.

At the edge of my vision, an arm appeared — male — then someone walked into the room, his back to me. For a second, panic hit me at the thought that it might be Hans. But this man was shorter, heavier, with an air of authority about him. I could not see his face, and after a few seconds he drifted out of view. Still no sign of Karen.

We waited. If only a couple of people were inside, we could probably break in and take charge. But a peek through a sliver of windowpane was not going to give us enough certainty about our opposition to justify the risk.

Then Jeff — bless his heart — renewed all the confidence I'd ever had in him. He kicked over a plant in a large ceramic pot. When it broke, it might as well have been a shotgun blast. We didn't have a chance. Before I could move, the sliding door to the deck slapped open and two floodlights went on right over our heads. A hand poked through the open door. It had a gun in it.

"You guys are amazing," a man's voice said. "Get in here."

We walked into a kitchen, a sense of déjà vu mixing with dread. He was short, on the heavy side, fortyish. I glanced at Jeff. He looked like his heart had been ripped out and only nervous tension was keeping him on his feet.

Ellen, who had finally been distracted from her magazine, stood beside the table, her mouth open, her eyes revealing a confused search for the right words. Jeff opened the conversation for her: "I trusted you."

"Phone him," the man snapped. Ellen

picked up the phone and dialed. Whoever was on the other end answered immediately.

"They got past you," she said. "It's secure for now, but get over here fast." Any lingering uncertainty I had about Ellen vanished.

"Where's my wife?" I said. It was like I'd dropped a bomb in the room. "Is she here?" They both just stood there, him with his gun, her clutching the folded magazine. "I want Karen!"

"Keep your voice down," Ellen said. "There's . . . there's an elderly lady living here. She owns the place, and she's sick." They seemed confused, as if caught by surprise in the middle of something far more complicated than it looked.

"Who's he?" I asked, looking at the middle-aged guy. My fear was gone, replaced by cold anger.

"I don't have to talk to you," he said. "I'm the one with the gun." He turned to Ellen. "See if he's here yet."

"Where's Karen?"

"Be quiet," Ellen hissed. "Phil, take them out on the deck."

But Phil never got a chance to do that. A voice, muffled and tired, said from the living room, "What's happening?" And Karen walked into the room. She looked terrible, her face white, hair mussed, eyes struggling for focus. Everyone froze as she stared at one face after another, until she settled on me.

"Karen."

Her face flooded with sudden recognition, and she swayed, shock contorting her features. I caught her before she fell and eased her down into a chair. Still sagging, she started making little gasping sounds, struggling for air.

"What did you do to her?" I shouted. "Jeff, find a phone and call an ambulance."

"No." The man Ellen had called Phil pointed his gun at me. "Settle down. She's all right."

"She's not all right!"

"Ben." Karen's voice was soft, almost inaudible, but somehow it cut through the loud voices. "Dead. Said you were . . ." The sound trailed away, and she stared, eyes unfocused.

Everyone stopped talking, making the knock on the door startling. Ellen went into the living room to answer it. Jeff and I waited, both sensing that this visitor would be bad news. He was.

Hans walked into the kitchen, followed by the cool guy. The little one whose shins had taken such a beating from Jeff wasn't with them.

"You people really slay me," Hans said, his voice filled with contempt. He wasn't speaking to Jeff and me.

"Us?" Phil said. "You were supposed to pick them up at the dock. They almost walked into the house. You messed up but good."

"I told you from the beginning we needed more people on this. What did you think I could do with two people?"

"There used to be three of you."

"Yeah, well the other guy didn't work out." Hans turned and stared at Jeff, then me. "I owe you one," he said, looking into my soul.

Phil beckoned to Ellen, and she walked over to him, her face reflecting nothing. I heard Phil tell her to put Karen back to bed.

"She's sick," I said.

"Shut up, Ben!" Phil grabbed my arm, Hans grabbed Jeff's, and we were herded into a bedroom. The door slammed behind us, and I heard Hans say from the other side, "Don't even think of trying to come out of there."

Inside the room, I turned and stared at Jeff. He wilted. I was tempted to hit him, but I figured just being Jeff was punishment enough. Anyone could have kicked over a plant, but I would have laid odds that Jeff would have been the one to do it. And he'd been totally wrong about Ellen. In fact, he had seemed a bit hurt, flashing her accusing looks while we talked in the kitchen. Maybe he'd had a thing for her.

"Sorry, Ben," he said. "I should have seen whatever I tripped over. And you were right about Ellen. Maybe I should have let you do this job alone." He stared at the floor, disgust with himself evident.

"No time for that," I said. "Check the window."

He did. "Locked."

"Unlock it."

"No, it's got a big Yale thing in the track. We'll have to break the glass."

"They'd be on to us too fast."

"So we wait here until they drag us out to shoot us somewhere?"

"I don't think so," I said, pondering. "Are you sure they still want to kill us? I mean, they told Karen I was dead. Now I'm alive. They're obviously holding her for some reason, and I think it made a big difference that she saw me."

"We still don't know what's going on. Are you going to risk your life on the possibility that Hans is in a better mood now than he was before?"

But I wasn't paying attention. Voices were coming through the door from the living room outside. I motioned for Jeff to keep quiet.

". . . stay under now?" Phil's voice.

"She should have been out till midnight. I made sure this time." Ellen.

"You kill her and the whole thing comes down."

"She's okay. So what do we do with them?"

"That's your fault, Hans." Phil. "She was never supposed to see him again."

Hans rumbled a protest. I missed the words.

"Get out. Go guard the perimeter or whatever." Hans left, slamming the door.

"Don't keep goading him, Phil," Ellen said. "It seems to me he's got a long memory."

"I'm the one paying him."

"And now we're in the soup. Was there so much risk that we couldn't hire two or three more people?"

"We're looking at kidnapping and murder, Ellen."

"And we're bunglers at both. This was a stupid idea."

"Oh yeah? Think about the alternative."

"Maybe he's already lost enough that nobody will believe him," Ellen said. I had no idea what that meant.

"We've got two more weeks, maybe less. Karen's our insurance, and up until tonight she had no idea she was a hostage. If he's got anything left, he could bring us down." Who were they talking about?

"Maybe she won't remember tonight. She was pretty dazed."

"You wish." Phil sounded bitter. "Now we've got to work it out all over again."

"It's getting too complicated, Phil. You're turning the whole thing into a zoo."

"We could walk away from it."

"Yeah, right."

They moved into the kitchen, and their voices faded. I would have tried the door, but the deadbolt on it could only be opened with a key.

THIRTEEN

"You need to know what's happening," Phil said. "I don't want anyone fouling up because of ignorance." We were in a van, Phil's I presumed, with Hans driving. Jeff and I were in the back seat, and Phil was holding his gun on us. Whether or not they had a route planned didn't seem to be important. We were simply driving so that Phil could talk. I watched the lights across the lake and willed someone to know that we were in the van, in desperate trouble again.

Karen had looked terrible. How could human beings turn a bright, alive, defenseless woman into a mumbling wreck and then say she was all right? I'd seen no signs of a deprogrammer — Phil didn't fit the bill. As soon as Karen was safely asleep again, and they'd finished their discussion in the kitchen, they'd hauled us out of the bedroom and taken us for a ride. Ellen and Hans's sidekick had stayed behind.

"Okay, Phil," I said, my voice cracking with fury. "Tell me that Jim Barker wanted to deprogram his daughter, so you snatched her to protect her from —"

"Can it, Sylvester."

"Tell me lots of stories, Phil! Make it good. I'll believe whatever you say."

"Shut up!" he shouted. "I'm going to tell you the truth."

I'd run out of steam. Jeff beside me reached out and gripped my arm hard. I got his message.

Phil hesitated, regrouping. "Ellen's my sister. I'm head of operations at Electar."

"So you're a criminal family," I said. "I'm impressed."

"Shut up, Ben," Jeff said again.

"I got Ellen in as Barker's executive secretary so she could keep the old guy from blind-siding me."

"About what?" I knew I was making it harder for him, but I couldn't help myself.

He thought about his words, as if he was about to move into dangerous territory. He was. "I've made contact with some people. Middle Eastern. Barker Electronics, among other things, makes guidance systems for U.S. armaments."

"You're selling secrets to the Arabs?"

"They pay better than the Chinese." Phil didn't seem to have lost any sleep over it.

"What have you sold them?"

"None of your business."

Phil had already revealed enough to show us that he didn't care, that he already had other plans for Jeff and me, terminal plans.

"What's the deal?" I asked. "We don't need to hear your dirty secrets."

"Get this clear, Sylvester," Phil said. "You too," waving his gun vaguely in Jeff's direction. "Karen doesn't know. She still thinks we snatched her to protect her from her father. We've told her she's been sick, and the sedation has messed up her sense of time."

"Why shouldn't she know you're slime?"

"That's our business. We have things that need to be done, and you two can hurt us. I want you to understand that this isn't small potatoes. We've got a big deal going on here."

"Big enough to send Hans to kill us?" I asked.

"It would have been easier if Stupid here hadn't botched it. But here you are."

"Karen's seen me. She'll remember."

"Maybe. We'll work that out later. For now, you need to understand that if you blow this deal —"

"How can we avoid it? We're still in the dark."

"Okay. We contacted Barker and told him we had his daughter."

"Why? Why kidnap her?"

"Barker caught on. He started an investigation. We thought Ellen had it stopped when he got his disease. She spread the word that he'd turned paranoid."

I was missing something. What disease? Jeff asked the question for me.

"Alzheimer's. Didn't you know? The old boy's got the big A."

I didn't. But for the moment I couldn't indulge myself in the complexities of poetic justice. "You kidnapped Karen to stop Barker from investigating?"

"Ben has a brain," Phil said. "We're waiting for a delivery from Barker — very important stuff." He paused. "Karen is not to know any of this. She's supposed to believe in us. Ellen and I are her friends."

"What if I tell her the truth?" I asked.

Phil turned to Hans. "Pull over. It's time to feed your little dream." Hans put the car on a widening of the shoulder and got out. Opening the back door, he grabbed an unsuspecting Jeff and dragged him out.

"I want you to understand this, Ben," Phil said as Jeff began to yell. The thumping sounds I heard didn't make sense until I realized that I was hearing fist hitting flesh.

"What are you doing?"

"I want to know for sure that you're going to do exactly what I say."

156

"Anything! Tell him to stop!"

"There's lots of time." He turned on the radio — a country station, some guy moaning about Sally who had done him wrong. Jeff was making animal sounds and saying "No" over and over.

"Stop it! I've got the message."

Phil reached over and tapped the horn. The thumping stopped, the back door opened, and Jeff fell across the seat. His face was a mess. I glanced at Hans staring in the window and was encouraged to see that one of his eyes was watery and starting to bruise.

Jeff groaned. "You didn't have to do that," I said angrily.

"I think it was helpful." Phil smirked, obviously deeply moved by Jeff's plight. "I've got you all mushy and ready to cooperate. You know, of course, that we don't really need this bag of bones" — pointing to Jeff — "so if you decide to get crafty, Hans will finish the job."

"Gratefully," Hans added.

I turned my attention to Jeff, who had managed to pull himself upright on the seat. There were only a couple of cuts, not deep. He'd be heavily bruised for days, but no facial bones looked obviously broken.

"Look somewhere else," Jeff muttered at me, his words slurred through swollen lips.

"Let me die in peace."

"No hard feelings, okay," Hans said, turning the car around and heading back in the direction of Electar.

The anger was bubbling, producing a dull ache behind my left eye, but I couldn't do anything to answer its craving. Locking my fingers around Phil's neck was not an option. Neither was jumping Hans and engineering a crash.

"What are we going to do now?" I asked. "Pull wings off some butterflies?"

"They're out of season," Phil said. "You're going back to Electar. This messy excuse for a human being" — meaning Jeff — "is going to be kept under lock and key elsewhere. Hans will watch him. Any disobedience from you and Hans gets to have his deepest wish come true."

Hans chuckled appreciatively. If it hadn't been so serious I would have laughed out loud at their bold attempt to reproduce the sleazy cruelty of 50's B-movies. It was obviously intended to keep us terror-stricken.

But I wasn't in the mood for amusement or terror. I wanted Karen and my kids out of there and back with me. And I wasn't prepared to be a victim. At the same time, I knew I'd have to be very careful or Jeff would disappear forever. Nothing I had learned about Hans led me to suspect he'd wimp out on an opportunity to complete his revenge.

They dropped Phil and me in Electar, and then Hans pulled away with Jeff in the back seat. Jeff had said nothing more. I wondered if his anger paralleled my own. It probably did, though neither of us had a way to vent it.

Phil led me back into the house. Ellen was waiting in the kitchen. Karen was probably still asleep, drugged into oblivion. I stared at Ellen for a moment, trying to fathom someone who could spin such webs of betrayal and then avoid any appearance of guilt. She looked so ordinary.

Phil was in no mood for chit-chat. He herded me into the spare bedroom and snapped the deadbolt behind him as he left. I was shut down for the night, alone.

Not many people have accused me of being deep. I live on the plane of action, not introspection. But as I lay on the halfway comfortable bed, I made a brave attempt to get in touch with myself, to figure out which emotions were just trauma and which would give me the resources to fight my way out of this. It would have been nice to be able to pray and get some sort of divine intervention out of it, but I wasn't ready to buy into religion.

So I muddled through my inventory, dismissing the adrenaline and the fear, feeling the power of the anger. Anger was dangerous, I knew. It could make me irrational. But I had little else. With my emotions catalogued, I went through the facts. They were bleak enough to send me into almost terminal depression — we were prisoners of people who would not hesitate to kill.

Even if I got Karen out of Electar, I wasn't sure how far I could move her. What drugs was she on? Was she hooked on them? Did rescuing Karen mean I had to abandon Jeff? Was he worth enough to me to risk my wife?

Jim Barker was an unknown quantity. I couldn't think of a more unlikely ally, but there he was. Of course, I had no idea how advanced the Alzheimer's was, if Phil had been telling the truth about that. Could he help us, or was he so far gone or so afraid for his daughter that he would do what he was told?

All of this thinking was pretty useless, I finally told myself. Karen and I were trapped, and rescuing her would involve so many layers of detail that it made little sense even to start plotting something. I'd always thought so much of my abilities, living by my wits in one culture after another. But now I had not the ghost of a strategy to offer.

I'd been frustrated beyond words by the impotence of my situation ever since Jeff poked a gun in my face back in Lynden. Whenever I got control of one part of this bizarre adventure, another part reached up and tried to smother me.

As I lay in the darkness, staring, unable to conceive of sleep, I ached for even five minutes with Karen. There had to be a way to get us out together, but I sensed that it would take more than wits to make it happen. As the hours passed, I began to crave the chance to talk to someone about it. But I was on my own. Finally, near dawn, I must have fallen asleep. My dreams gave me no encouragement at all.

FOURTEEN

Morning. I awoke disoriented, a dull sense of hopelessness smothering my mind with gray fog. Gradually things came into focus. I turned, looking first at the locked window, then at the bolt on the door. For a few seconds I sank deeper under the blankets, pillow over my head, denial percolating in my bones.

Then the door snapped open and Phil stood there. "Get up. Ellen doesn't like spreading breakfast all over the morning." I got up.

"What's to stop me from bolting out of here first chance I get?" I asked.

"How much do you like your pal?" he responded.

"Not much."

"But enough."

I turned my back and walked into the bathroom. The shower did little except to confirm to me that I was awake. There wasn't much point in getting wonderfully scrubbed up, because I had to wear the same clothes I'd put on the day before.

As I dressed, I let my mind run through the possibilities again. But my list was short — I could grab Karen and smash my way out of the place (past Phil, Ellen, and Hans's sidekick). In that case, Jeff would die. Or I could play out Phil's game, do whatever he told me to. And maybe all of us would die.

I already knew the answer. Jeff, for all his annoying inconsistencies and the blunder on the deck, was still human. I could do something wild and end his life or play it safe and maybe get all of us killed. The odds were miserable, but I wasn't prepared to play fast and loose with the guy's life.

There was a sharp rap on the door. "You drown in there, Ben?" Phil asked. I came out. Phil and Hans's pal — I think his name was Harold — were waiting. No guns were obvious. They didn't think they needed to persuade me further.

Phil sat me down in the living room. Ellen was standing beside the front window, saying nothing. "Here's the deal, Ben. Karen's due to wake up in a couple of hours. When she does, we'll find out whether or not she remembers seeing you last night. If she remembers, we'll try to convince her that it was her imagination. You better pray she remembers. As far as I'm concerned, I hope she doesn't."

"If she doesn't remember, I'll disappear. Jeff will go too." I was surprised at my calm.

"Sorry." He wasn't.

"If she remembers —"

"Then you talk to her. Tell her she's been sick. Say Ellen wanted to hide her from her father, but when she got sick, Ellen got scared and phoned you. I don't care what you tell her as long as Ellen and I come up smelling like roses. She's never supposed to know that we kidnapped her to silence her old man. If she finds out, you die anyway."

They fed me breakfast, some kind of cereal that had turned at least one sawdust manufacturer into the owner of a castle in the south of France. I ate with difficulty. Then they herded me back into the bedroom, throwing half a dozen old *Reader's Digest*s in after me.

I waited, reading occasionally, pacing often. Lunch came — door unlocked, arm pushed in with a plate of something at the end of it, door locked. I ate sitting on the bed. No one came for the dirty plate.

It was 3:08 by my watch when Phil came into the room and shut the door behind him.

"Well?" I said.

"Congratulations. You get to live — for now. Karen remembered that she saw you

164

last night. We couldn't persuade her otherwise."

"Is she all right?"

"Sure. We're letting her come down off the drugs."

"How long before I can see her?" The word *drugs* had made me furious again.

"Couple of hours. We want her fully awake. In the meantime, get your story right."

I thought about it, pacing again after Phil had left and bolted the door. This was my one shot. Either I pulled it off now or I might as well open an artery. Most of it depended on how alert Karen was.

When they finally let me out, I discovered that I was afraid to talk to Karen. Not of what I would say, but just of seeing her, communicating with her. What was most frightening was the memory of her video. When I'd watched her on the television at Dave's house, I'd seen right into her soul, with no barriers at all. Was it an illusion, a trick of the camera? Or was I about to talk to a stranger?

They sat me down in the living room, then Ellen led Karen in and directed her to an armchair opposite me, four feet between us. She looked so pale in the scruffy housecoat they'd given her. I wanted everyone else to leave, but the thought hadn't entered their minds.

"Hi," she said, her voice thin, soft.

"Hi," I said.

"They said you were dead."

A burst of fury came ripping through me. I must have gone white, but I managed to control it.

"A mistake. Some other guy named Sylvester. Ellen finally checked for sure, and here I am." I smiled awkwardly, and she smiled in response.

"I've been sick."

"Do you know what happened to you?"

She hesitated, thinking. "My father wanted to deprogram me. Ellen got me out. We took everything, so Dad would think I'd moved. But I've been sick." She'd bought it — the whole phony story. But I wasn't prepared for her next words: "Did you look after the cat, Ben?"

I waited too long before I said, "Sure. He's as frisky as ever. Jeff's brother Dave is looking after him."

I began to look at her eyes as we talked, as she told me about the great care our kids were getting nearby. She didn't mention the name of the place, so she probably didn't know it. But her eyes were wide open and the barriers had vanished. She spoke quietly, yet there was a confident assurance in her that I'd never seen before. Ever.

She looked so thin, weak, like a gentle shadow that could be snuffed out with the smallest beam of light. Chances were she'd collapse if she tried to walk a block. Whatever they'd used on her had wasted her away physically, though mentally she'd lost nothing. Probably they had just kept her asleep most of the time.

Then, just as the small talk was thinning, she said, "Last night Jeff was with you. Where is he now?"

Phil tensed, signaling me frantically with his eyes. I hesitated deliberately, trusting her to carry the ball. "He, uh, went back home. Even accountants get only so much holiday time. Since you're safe, he didn't think he'd be needed anymore."

"But he had five weeks off, Ben. I haven't been here that long." She'd picked up on the story I'd created for Jeff, who wasn't an accountant. "Is something going on here I don't know about?"

Careful, my eyes warned. I took her hand. "Look, Karen, Jeff ran into some trouble. I didn't want to tell you until you were better."

"What happened?" she asked. Phil looked ready to burst an artery.

"He's been under a lot of stress. Last night he went back on the booze. Some dive downtown in Kelowna. A couple of guys beat him up in an alley."

She put her hand up to her mouth. "Where is he? Did you get a doctor?"

"Phil took care of it," I said, treasuring the way my words made the veins stand out on the side of Phil's head. I waited.

"Yeah," Phil mumbled. "He'll be okay."

"Is he in a hospital?"

"No," I said, before Phil could break in. "Motel room."

"Then can't we bring him here?"

Perfect. She'd suspected Jeff was being held elsewhere, and our enemies were desperate to keep Karen believing in them. I was beginning to see that there were ways to play that to our advantage. My master's degree in political science wouldn't go to waste after all.

"If I'm staying with Karen now," I said to Phil, "Jeff could stay in the bedroom I was in. He's got money to pay for his own food. It sure beats recuperating in a motel room." Phil glared at me, and I suspected I might have to suffer someday for my bold move.

"Sure," Phil said. "I'll get someone to bring him over." He used the phone in his own bedroom — probably Hans was getting full instructions on telling Jeff to keep his mouth shut.

As far as I was concerned, the key was just to get Jeff into the same house with us. It was a cinch that Hans would stay outside now that Karen was alert. Even Hans's sidekick Harold had faded into obscurity. I hadn't seen him since morning.

I looked at Karen, and when our eyes met, there was a connection that locked us together. We were fighting back. Together. Karen and I. And even though I had no plan, I was certain now that we were going to win. She'd changed dramatically — not just the drugs but her new open clarity. The fears I'd had about losing her to her religion were fading.

It was twenty minutes before Jeff arrived. He came in alone, with only a hint of an unsteady walk. But his face was a disaster, one eye blue-black, the other tending to shades of yellow and green. His left cheek was purple and his lower lip had split. It hurt just to look at him.

"You okay, Jeff?" I said.

Karen stared at him, trying to keep it together. I watched her struggle with her anger and mask it with a look of baffled concern. The new Karen was amazing. After almost a month of being kept in a virtual coma, she was in control of herself and in tune with what was happening. I felt certain I could trust her to follow my lead if an opportunity opened up.

"Stupid of me to go back on the bottle. Even stupider to walk down an alley," he said, speaking carefully to minimize the pain. As far as I knew, Jeff had never been a drinker. Hans had coached him well on my made-up explanation for his injuries.

"Pretty wild behavior for an accountant, Jeff," Karen said. "I thought you'd stay on the wagon."

Jeff's eyes widened, but he said nothing. Phil didn't have a clue what was going on.

Everything moved into a stalemate as we stared at each other, awkward. Karen had single-handedly gotten Jeff out of his hostage situation and let him know that she understood who the bad guys were. Phil might still have the upper hand, but we were encroaching on him. The weak link in his armor was his desire to fool Karen. As long as he was convinced that Karen thought her dad was the villain, he'd give us a lot of leeway. If he found out she knew that he and Ellen were the monsters, we'd be finished.

Then Karen upped the ante. "I've been sick, Jeff. What did the doctor say I had, Phil?"

Phil was quick. "The doctor said it was some water bacterium — beaver fever, he called it." I'd never heard of it, but later I found out that it's a real disease that creates stomach problems. Phil was taking risks on our ignorance.

"I'm better. Do we really have to stay here? It seems like years since I've been home."

"Your father wants to deprogram you."

"Ben's here now. What can my father do?"

"Give it another week, Karen," Phil said. "Ellen's been softening him up by phone."

"Does he know where I am?"

"Of course not."

"What has Ellen been telling him?" There was a dangerous edge to Karen's voice now.

"That you've gone into hiding because you're afraid of him. That you contacted Ellen from your hiding place and begged her to intervene with your dad. You're frightened. It's not right that a father should persecute his adult daughter like this."

"Is he listening?"

"I think so," Ellen said. She'd faded so much into the background beside Phil's dominance that I'd almost forgotten she was in the room. "Give it a week, Karen."

"What if he traces your calls?" I asked.

"We relay them through the head office in

Cleveland. Besides, we've told him that Karen isn't actually with us. Jim's in Arizona for the winter." Ellen appeared confident with her blatant lies, and I decided to rattle her.

"What was Barker's plan for snatching Karen?"

She stayed cool. "He had people to do it. They were supposed to bring her to Arizona on the strength of a letter from her dad. The kids would stay at some sort of dude ranch."

"How could he be sure I'd be out of the picture?"

"You're not home much anyway." That stung a bit. "But Jim's got an inside track into the company you work for. He knew exactly where you were." Somebody's head was going to roll for that.

"So how did you beat him to Karen?"

"He told me all about his plan. We got into action before his people could."

So plausible. Too bad it was all a lie. I waited for Jeff to interrupt and blow the whole thing, but he seemed to be clued in to the deception and he kept his mouth shut.

We now had everyone together except our children. Obviously Karen wasn't about to sanction us making a move for freedom until the kids were safe. Phil showed every evidence that common decency and compassion would never stand in the way of covering up his crimes.

"I miss the kids," Karen said. "As long as we need to stay here a week, they could sleep in our room."

"There's nothing here for them to play with," Phil murmured.

"There must be other kids in this town," Karen objected. "A playground. We can buy a few toys."

"They're having such a great time at the resort."

"They're only little kids, Phil." Karen was using the voice that usually got her what she wanted. She used it rarely, but when she did it was very effective.

"We're booked into the resort for three more days. Really, they'll be safer and happier there than here. I have to insist."

His eyes were steel, accepting no objections. I felt a chill, knowing that these people still had us under their control. Phil's icy cruelty was something he wore like a comfortable old sweater.

I looked at Karen and saw defeat in her eyes. "I'm tired. Ben, can we go and get some sleep?"

"Go ahead," Phil said, throwing me a look of warning. He had my kids, after all.

When we got into the bedroom, Karen

started to talk, but I signaled her with an up-raised hand. There were few places in the room where they could have hidden the bug, so I found it quickly, inside a lamp-shade. Rather than crushing it, I left it alone. Phil would just replace a broken one anyway.

Instead, we kept up a running conversation as if we believed everything Phil and Ellen had told us. All the while we communicated by writing, each of us explaining what we knew, putting forward every crazy idea we could think of to get out of this. Finally, with nothing much to show for our brainstorming, we slept. Once, late in the night, I heard someone padding around outside — Hans or the sidekick.

It was one more reminder that our enemies still held most of the cards.

FIFTEEN

I woke early, the sun glinting through a gap in the curtain. The room was cold, probably reflecting a downsweep of Arctic air from Alaska. Karen was beside me, and for a moment the past month vanished and we were home, catching a few extra moments before the kids got up. But the illusion vanished as I came fully awake. We were still prisoners of Phil, Ellen, Hans, and the sidekick, Harold.

Karen mumbled in her sleep, her face still far too pale, too thin. I watched her for a few minutes, remembering all the reasons why she meant so much to me, why the search for her had been worth it. Then she opened her eyes, bewilderment fading to happy recognition.

I moved closer so that I could whisper right in her ear. "Don't forget the bug. Be careful what you say."

She moved alongside so we could whisper in each other's ears. "We have to get the kids," she said.

"They're safe for now. Even someone as rotten as Phil wouldn't want to hurt children. Where would it get him?"

"Forget it, Ben. I know you. If you get the chance you'll make a break for it and risk the kids. Please don't even think about it."

"I'm not some selfish monster."

"I never said you were. Just don't make them pawns in all of this."

"I love my kids."

"You hardly know them. Look, Ben, I don't want to get into this, but I'm not sure you're thinking enough about their safety. You're planning some big play to save yourself and me and maybe Jeff. What then? Do we hope and pray Phil and Ellen won't send us the boys' ears in the mail?"

"I've thought about it a lot. These creeps might use Jeff to control us, but the kids? If we could get away and call the police, they'd have no reason to make things harder on themselves by harming our children."

"Ben, I'm begging you."

All right, so I was taking a hard line. Regret is easy after the fact, but I really believed I knew what I was doing. This wasn't some kind of power trip. Sure, I'd gotten used to making decisions for Karen. But over the past day I'd weighed the options, and there was only one viable solution — look for a crack in their defenses and get out of there.

"Don't you see that they're going to kill me?" I went on. "For some reason they want you to think they're on the side of the angels. But they know I know all about them. It's obvious they've got to bump me off. The only reason I'm not dead yet is that you saw me alive. The first chance they have to stage an accident and you're a widow."

"I know the risk," she said. "But why can't we wait? Maybe a chance will come up without putting the boys in danger."

"We can't afford to wait. Jeff and I are both expendable, and Phil isn't telling us what kind of time line he's using. It's not just for me, Karen. If I'm dead, who knows what they're going to do to you eventually."

"Please, Ben." But I wasn't prepared to listen. All the evening before, while we'd passed notes to one another, I'd become more and more convinced that we had no hope unless we acted right away. Sure there was some risk to the kids, but the alternative was to make them orphans. Karen's pleading was shaking me to the core, but I had to do what made sense to me.

"Ben, don't do it." She was crying, and I did feel like a monster. "You have no right to risk their lives."

"They'll be all right. Do you have a better idea?"

"Prayer," she said, her whispered voice broken. "God will help us. We've got a few days. He's already helped us."

"How?"

"Do you really think I got through that routine yesterday by myself?" The tears were drying, and her whisper was getting stronger. "Please understand, Ben. Things are different now. I can feel things. I can assert myself — maybe not very well, but it's getting better. You've been my protector when I needed it, but you had to know it wasn't healthy, that I had to move on. I've been searching so long . . ."

"Why didn't you ever tell me?"

"You were too busy playing the white knight. Honestly, Ben, when I left Lynden, I could just picture you chasing after me and getting yourself killed. You love this — poor helpless Karen and macho Ben. But I don't want to be helpless any more."

"Is this some kind of power trip, you and God? You turn yourself over to him and he makes you stronger than Supergirl?"

We were glaring at each other, face to face, bodies tense. Then she looked away. "It's not power," she said. "All I wanted was to be the person I was made to be, not some basketcase afraid of her own shadow and useless to my husband and children."

"So what's your option?"

"Wait and pray. We're so close to having everyone here. Surely if we get the kids back, we can overcome Phil and Ellen."

"What about Hans and Harold?"

"Who?"

"Two toughs — Hans and Harold. They're the ones who tried to kill me. Hans is the guy who beat up Jeff last night. And right now they're spelling each other patrolling the yard."

"That's why Phil looks so smug about all this."

"And that's why I have to act the moment I see an opening."

"No, Ben." She clung to me. "The children —"

"Will be okay."

"No they won't. These people are degenerates. They'll hurt the kids for revenge."

"Their first goal is to kill us — Jeff and me."

I got up. There was no reason to go on with this. I was going to act when I got the chance; there weren't any other options.

"Don't. Please." I waited, her whisper echoing too loudly in the room. "Ben." I waited. "Tell me that you love your children."

"I love my children."

"Please, Ben."

There was nothing more to say. I got dressed.

When we went into the kitchen to search out breakfast, we found Phil and Jeff sitting, staring everywhere except at each other. Jeff's face looked worse than ever.

"How are you doing?" Karen said to Jeff, her voice soft, caring.

"Better. That . . . uh, those guys at the bar really put me through the wringer."

Phil scowled at the small talk.

"Where's Ellen?" I asked.

"Shopping in Kelowna."

"Who's going to make breakfast?"

"Not me. Are cereal and milk beyond you people?"

"I want eggs."

"There's the fridge, there's the stove. Eat yourself to death." Phil's good mood and high spirits sure cheered me up.

"Cooking oil?" I asked as I got the eggs and some bacon.

"Use the bacon grease."

"Come on, Phil. You got some oil?"

"First cupboard." Phil did a half turn with his chair and picked up a newspaper, his face in profile.

Grabbing the oil, I poured a bit in the frying pan. I turned to Jeff and said, "Kind of reminds you of Sylvester Road . . . waiting up in the dark for bad guys."

"What?" he said.

"You never know what might happen. A good breakfast could put it all right."

He still looked puzzled, but I had his attention. Phil was ignoring us. It was time to make our play.

The range was gas fired. As I picked up the oil again, I glanced at Phil. He was buried in his paper. I dumped oil on a burner set on high, and it went up with a woof, scorching my fingers.

Phil threw aside the newspaper and came at me as I grabbed the curtains, ripped them down, and flung them on the fire. Jeff met Phil halfway and sent him flying with a well-connected right hook. One more blow put Phil out of the action as the flames started inching up the wall.

I threw in Phil's newspaper for good measure, then opened the French doors at the back of the house and yelled, "Fire!" Fortunately, it was Harold outside, not Hans, and we met him as he ran inside. It was my turn, and I decked him with a quick right and then a left.

I turned to Karen as smoke began to form like a heavy inverted cone hung from the ceiling. She was leaning against the kitchen table, her hand over her mouth.

"Get our coats," I told her. "We have to get out." She just stared at me. "Jeff," I shouted, "get our coats." The flames had moved along the cupboards. Jeff came back with heavy clothing. Our boots and Karen's shoes were at the back door. Phil was moving weakly on one side of the kitchen floor. Harold was groaning, face down, on the other side.

I grabbed Karen's hand and started toward the door. She was dazed and didn't resist. "What about them?" Jeff shouted.

"Leave them. They're both conscious."

"Wait!" he shouted. I stopped as he ran over to Phil and shook him. Phil swung at him blindly. Jeff tried to drag him out, but he struggled.

"Leave him," I said. "I'm taking Karen." We were all coughing now, the flames eating into the ceiling. I pulled Karen through the glass door at the back. Jeff came after, dragging Harold. We scrambled down the steps to the lawn, Jeff giving Harold a bumpy ride before dropping him on the grass about twenty feet from the house. Harold was out of it. We threw on our coats — it was cold, clouds coming in rapidly above us.

"Phil didn't make it out!" Jeff shouted at me. I was pulling Karen toward the front of the house, but he grabbed my coat.

"He's still in there!"

I looked at the house. The kitchen area was sheeted with flames. "He's okay," I said. "If he has any sense, he's headed toward the front door."

"Listen to him, Ben," Karen said. "Phil could have been overcome with the smoke." Her voice was tense, breaking.

"Let go of my jacket." Jeff let go, and I took Karen's hand and ran around to the front. Just behind me I could hear Jeff, his breathing labored. Obviously he'd gotten more smoke than I had. The front door was shut tight.

Jeff rushed at the door and hit it hard, but the combination of solid core and deadbolt stopped him cold. Panting, his shoulder obviously hurting, he turned and looked around, then grabbed a lawn ornament — some kind of gnome — and threw it through the front window.

"You're crazy!" I yelled at him. "The creep wants to kill us. He's not worth it."

Trust Jeff not to make sense. He flung some pieces of cold metal into my hand — car keys — and said calmly, "Everybody God made is worth it." Then he was through the window.

"Help him, Ben," Karen said, clutching my sleeve and pulling me toward the window. Heavy smoke was coming out of the house.

"No way."

"You started this. Do you really want to kill somebody?"

The violence of the flames was horrifying, but hard as it may be to believe, I didn't want to kill anyone. I climbed through the window and dropped to the floor. Visibility was a problem. I took off my coat and pulled a sleeve across my mouth and nose.

"Jeff!" I shouted, my voice muffled. Carefully, I crawled forward, coughing, the coat as a shield, my eyes burning, tears blinding me. The kitchen was twenty feet away, flames showing through the smoke. There wasn't much time left to do anything.

There he was — Jeff — crawling backward, dragging Phil out of the fire, impossibly close to the source of heat. How he could have stood it, I'll never know. For myself, I couldn't get closer than ten feet from him.

It happened so sudden I couldn't have hoped to reach him. With a crack, the whole ceiling in the hallway came down, powered by an enormous trunk someone had put in the crawl space above the ceiling joists. The two men disappeared, and a sheet of flame swung out and backhanded me across the room.

Did I hear a scream? Did Jeff struggle to free himself from the rubble? I don't know. It was all confusion and so hot that the skin on my hands and face was starting to cook. Jeff and Phil were gone. I couldn't get anywhere near them. Hopeless, I scrambled out alone.

SIXTEEN

The snow was falling harder, the wipers having trouble keeping up. It would have been bad enough without the snow, Karen beside me a crumbled lump, hoping, no doubt praying, that we would get to the kids in time. If she would have said something, if she would have blamed me and told me the whole stupid idea was mine, I might have been able to wrestle with the pain. But she said nothing.

It was insane. We'd been free and clear, but Jeff had to make one last hero's rush, and now he was dead. I killed him . . . or he did it to himself . . . or —

When we'd seen it was pointless to try to rescue Jeff, let alone Phil, I'd grabbed Karen's hand, and we'd run for the rental car in the parking lot at the leisure center. Fortunately no one had moved it. We were intent on more than just getting out of there. Karen had spotted a brochure to a guest ranch outside of Vernon and had snatched it off the fridge as we were running from the house. Maybe the kids were there, maybe not, but I was determined not to put them at any more risk than I had.

Okay — I admit it. The fire was my fault. I started it. People died. I put my kids at risk. Jeff was gone. I didn't care a fig for Phil, but the image of the ceiling falling kept replaying like a video loop that no one could turn off. Fire and heat and roaring and the ceiling coming down and Jeff gone.

There was no need. I told him not to do it, but he was trapped in gung-ho mode, spaced out in some other world. There was no way to stop him short of knocking him cold. It was your fault, Jeff, not mine.

The video kept playing. Turn it off! Your fault, Jeff. No one made you do it.

After fifteen minutes on the road, Karen stirred. "How much farther?" Her voice was flat, as if she'd just awakened from a coma.

"We have to get to Vernon. North. Then east up into the hills. I don't know, maybe three-quarters of an hour."

"Are you sure about . . ." She stopped. "Did you see Jeff?"

"He's dead, Karen. I can't bring him back."

"I begged you not to."

"Don't." My voice broke, surprising me. Tears were blinding me, and a quick wipe with the back of my hand did nothing.

"It's all right," she whispered, but it wasn't all right. Between the snow and the film of water over my eyes, it was a miracle I didn't go off the winding road.

"We have to save the kids," she said. Maybe she suspected I was thinking of just turning the wheel and letting the car roll down the hillside into oblivion.

"I killed him."

"No. It's all right."

"You told me not to make the play."

"Let's worry about the kids."

The snow was getting deeper, about an inch on the road, two on the shoulders. It was only early December. Maybe God was sending me a message for killing one of his children. *This was insane!* I banged the steering wheel with my fist, the image of Jeff under a ball of flame flashing like a strobe through my mind.

"Don't take it on yourself, Ben."

"I have to phone his brother."

"Wait till we find the kids," she said.

"Dave left Jeff in my hands. I was supposed to take care of him."

"He made the choice to go back in."

"Why did he? Tell me that."

"I don't know . . . responsibility I guess. Phil wouldn't have been down if Jeff hadn't hit him."

"The guy deserved to be hung. Why bother with him?"

"Jeff told you before he went in."

"Nobody would give up his life to save someone who had beat him up, tried to kill him."

"Jeff may have been weak and futile in many ways, but he was a follower of Christ. You won't understand him, Ben, not the way you are now."

I could have pursued it, but I decided to shut up. Karen lay back against the headrest and seemed to be asleep. I doubted she was.

We rounded the northern head of Okanagan Lake and went into Vernon, Karen with her eyes clenched shut beside me. The snow was two inches deep on the pavement now, though none of the hardy Okanagan drivers seemed unduly upset about it.

I didn't kill Jeff. The fool ran back in to save a sack of garbage when he was free and clear. And I did go after Jeff. There was nothing more I could do. But I started the fire. Can't you see that Phil would have killed us anyway? He was a monster who brutalized women, kidnapped children, had husbands killed — he deserved it, and I could have cheered when the roof fell in on him. But Jeff was under it too. And I killed Jeff.

We climbed into the hills, the snow deepening. A plow had been through just before, and I took advantage of the near new tires on the small car I was driving. Karen was frightened, tense, but she said nothing. She knew we had to get there before our captors got to the kids. Ellen, Hans, and Harold were still alive and dangerous.

I hoped I was on the right road. Not that I could muster any anxiety, but we couldn't afford to take the time to retrace our path. Karen had resumed her semi-coma state, as if she were reaching inside to neutralize the horror of the past few hours.

"You okay?" I said.

She stirred, opened her eyes. "No."

"You can't possibly hate me as much as I hate myself." My words sounded stupid, like a cute line from some crummy movie.

"I never said I hate you. I told you not to take chances, and you did. But you didn't kill Jeff. He probably would have destroyed himself some way or other before we were through with this."

"So we blame Jeff?"

Her eyes filled with tears. I saw it because I made a point of looking at her after I asked the question. "Why blame anyone? It happened."

Common sense told me to shut up. There

were too many raw emotions operating, and I didn't know how to read Karen anymore. She had this new strength, an ability to face what had to be faced. I'd never seen that before.

The road continued to wind upward. According to the brochure, this ranch where the kids might be offered year-round recreation. Presumably the attraction at the moment would be tobogganing.

As we drove, I began changing mental gears, pulling on my father hat. I was supposed to be a father, after all. Not much of a father. No kind of father at all. Would they have despised me if they knew what I'd done in the name of escape? Had I killed them too?

When we arrived, the place was impressive — crafted stone gates and a heated driveway that remained black and wet despite six inches of white stuff everywhere else. It was a big operation, more of a conference center than a ranch — large building at the front, smaller units built like log cabins on either side and stretching back several hundred yards. There was a prominent corral to the right, with a high-tech looking barn beside it.

No one was outside. We pulled up to the main building, and Karen was out of the door before I could shut off the engine. There was a reception desk inside, such as you would see in a hotel.

Karen took the initiative. "I'm here to pick up my kids. Karen Sylvester." I wondered where she got the energy and the appearance of normalcy.

The clerk was young, about twenty. She frowned, and I felt the first pang. "I don't remember anyone by that name." She hit a few keys on her computer. "We've only got about fifteen guests right now and no Sylvester."

"Two boys, one five, one seven."

"Mrs. Blake. She checked out half an hour ago. Two boys. Jack and —"

"Jimmie," Karen finished, her voice desperate. She turned to me, and her look of terror and accusing anger withered my soul.

"What was her name?"

"Blake."

"What did she look like?"

The clerk hesitated. "I don't know you. Our guests don't appreciate us revealing information about them to —"

"She kidnapped our children. Tell us." Karen's eyes were flaming enough to curl the toes of a heavyweight boxer. The clerk folded.

"About forty. Ordinary looking. I knew

they weren't her boys."

"How?"

"The youngest one told me a couple of days ago that he missed his mom. Apparently you were sick."

"Yes."

"Which way did they go?" I asked.

"No idea."

"Did she leave an address?"

"At check-in. Here. 519 Maple Lane. In Electar."

"Do you happen to know if she got a call before she left?"

"Yes. A few minutes before actually. Funny thing — she looked real upset, like something bad had happened but she had to smother her emotions about it."

"Call the police," Karen said.

"No police," I said, feeling a stab of panic that almost froze me to the floor.

"Enough of this, Ben. I'm calling them. If you want to run off and hide before they get here, go ahead." Her jaw was set, quivering slightly. I was amazed.

"The police will only increase the risk to our kids. Ellen hasn't got much to lose now. And do you know what the cops will mean for me? Don't you remember what happened this morning?" I caused it. People died.

"You can't run from it forever, Ben. If you'd called them before you came after me, maybe you wouldn't have people's lives on your account now." She saw the pain in my eyes and backed off. "I'm sorry," she said. "I had no right."

It was too much to take, her looking at me like that. I turned away and crossed the lobby to stare at the snow outside. Phil's wife had my kids. I couldn't bury it anymore, like the stupid snow that covered everything with a false white. I'd killed Phil. I'd killed Jeff. And now probably I'd killed my children. It was time to face it, to bring in the police.

Behind me, I could here Karen talking to the cops on the phone, crying, trying to make herself understood through the tears. And I was crying too, staring at the snow, crushed under the guilt and the fear for my boys.

There was one more job to do: Phone Dave Mancuso and tell him that his brother was dead. It was as awful as I thought it would be — me stumbling over words that never should have had to be said, them asking questions, revealing pain beyond imagining. All the while, I was diminishing, shrinking in on myself, down to the cold center where there was nothing but pain.

There was no need for a facade anymore, for bravado. If I could have drummed up the faith, I might have even mustered the courage to pray. But all I had was the loneliness of my chaotic thoughts. It wasn't enough.

SEVENTEEN

The cops in Canada were more polite than their American counterparts, but they lacked nothing in efficiency. We told them everything — Ellen's scheme to snatch Karen and the kids, my kidnapping by Jeff, the first episode with Hans, the escape, Electar, the fire, our kids.

I had no more strength left to protect us from the law, to try to solve it myself. Even my customary self-centeredness was evaporating under the urgency of getting my kids out of these monsters' hands. But there was no way for us to find out where they were.

Karen was strong through all the explanations. I was a basketcase, stumbling over words, getting time sequences confused.

The police had gotten the woman's license number from the hotel records. Phil's wife was driving, but she would have had time to switch cars and be well on her way to wherever she was planning to go.

Though the cop in charge had much more on his plate than he wanted to deal with, he took it on without much sign that it might be beyond him. The first concern was the kids. Presumably Ellen had come home or Hans had shown up early for his shift or Hans's sidekick had phoned him. One of them had called Phil's wife and she'd left the scene with our kids.

But where to? Obviously Electar was out — the fire would have drawn too much attention, and Karen and I knew the town was their base of operations. The main highways in the valley ran north and south, but there was a secondary highway east of Vernon and another east of Kelowna. Either one could take a fugitive hundreds of miles away in a few hours.

"It's too late for roadblocks," the cop told me, trying not to reveal the obvious fact that the situation was probably hopeless. "You and your wife need to establish a base in case these people call you."

"Where?" I asked.

"Here. It's the only point of contact you've got."

"Look, officer, we've got nothing to bargain with. The only reason they snatched Karen and the kids was to keep Jim Barker from calling a news conference or going to the police."

"I would have expected them to try to flee the country. They had no hope of being able to hold your wife forever."

"If you're asking me why they're still around, I don't know why."

"Any indication of what their next step might be?"

"There is no next step." I walked to the window. It was snowing again. "We've reached the end. Barker has the evidence — they have the kids."

The cop turned to Karen. "What do you think your father will do now?"

"We have to call him." Her voice was hollow. "He has to come here."

"He's got Alzheimer's, Karen," I said. "Who knows how he'll handle this?"

"My mom's okay. She'll guide him."

"It's worth a try," the cop said. "The evidence might be a bargaining chip. At the very least you've got to keep Mr. Barker from releasing the evidence before your children are safe. At this point, these people have considerable reason for a grudge against you two."

He didn't have to say it. The implication was plain. Because I'd taken things into my own hands, two people were dead and the rest of our enemies were angry enough to do just about anything.

"And what about Ben?" Karen's question was sudden and surprised me. "Are you going to charge him?"

"I can't give you a final answer on that," the cop said. He was fortyish, obviously higher up in the organization than the other two who were with him. "You came into the country under some measure of duress, and the person who brought you is dead. I suppose Customs and Immigration wouldn't have much choice but to give you the benefit of the doubt." He paused.

"The fire," I said.

"Yeah, the fire's going to be more of a problem. You were being held captive and your lives were at stake. But two people died. There'll be an inquest for sure. Until then, I have to know exactly where you are. That means you stay here. Ski season's starting soon, so we better make sure they have a room for you."

"First my father," Karen said.

"Can you reach him?" I asked.

"I think he's in Arizona like Ellen said. If not, I've got other numbers."

I passed her my calling card, and she went off to the hotel desk. When she was out of earshot, I asked the cop what he thought the chances were. He started into the expected nonsense about doing everything he could, but I stopped him cold.

"They've got good reason to kill my kids, don't they?"

"People in this kind of situation don't kill children, Mr. Sylvester. They use them as bargaining tools."

"Do you really think they'll call?"

"Unless they've gone totally off the deep end, they still want Jim Barker's evidence. They had your wife. Now they have your kids."

It made sense. I willed myself to believe it as I watched Karen walk back from the desk.

"Any luck?"

"He's in Arizona. I reached the maid, and she said he and Mom would be back at six."

"Is he rational?"

"I don't know. The maid wouldn't give out any information, even to me."

"Will your dad be prepared to turn over his evidence to save our kids?"

"Ben!" her face darkened. "Do you really think —"

"No. I have to believe he'll cooperate. There's nothing else."

"You hate him, don't you."

"No." She glared at me. "Yes," I said. "He's a monster."

"Look, folks, could you deal with this later?" The cop was getting impatient. "I want to bring in some equipment to monitor calls."

"They can't suspect the police are involved or we're cooked," I said. "Up to this point nobody's reported any kidnappings or attempted murders. If Ellen finds out the cops are listening, she'll have nothing more to lose."

Patiently, the cop handed me his card. "My name is on it. If you want to call my superior to find out whether or not I'm competent, please do so." I read the card — *Corporal Blakeny.*

"No need," I said. "I'm just asking you to be careful. You can monitor phone calls but I don't want anybody moving in on Ellen or Hans until my kids are safe."

"We've got lots of experience, Mr. Sylvester. In a case like this, the safety of your children is priority one." Blakeny's voice softened. "I've got two kids under ten myself."

"Ben?" Karen sounded tired. "If you don't mind, I'm going to book a room and lie down for awhile. Goodness knows how I'm going to sleep until —" Her voice broke and she walked across the lobby to the main desk.

"What do you want me to do?" I asked Corporal Blakeny.

"Stay with your wife, Mr. Sylvester. As soon as the phone equipment arrives, we'll set it up and do a few practice runs. Until then, just rest."

I followed Karen up to the room. She unlocked it with one hand and took my hand with the other. Her hand was warm but dry, almost feverish, as if she was burning immense amounts of energy. Inside the room, she clung to me so hard that my ribs hurt. "Stay close, Ben," she said. "Don't go."

"There's nowhere to go."

Finally, pulling away slowly, she sat in an armchair and shut her eyes. I waited, watching her, hoping she'd be able to hang on through the rest of this. When she spoke again, her voice was stronger, but she wasn't speaking to me:

"Help us. We can't do anything now but trust you. Don't take our kids from us. I couldn't live if anything . . ." She trailed off. I'd never heard a prayer like it, as if God was sitting next to her and she was revealing her deepest need; no pretense, no doubt.

"Do you want to talk to me?" I asked when her silence told me she was finished. I was uncertain with her.

"Guess so. We have to plan. For one thing, what am I going to ask my father to do?"

"Get up here with his evidence. We've got to have it all, nothing held back."

"Then we wait for Ellen to call?"

"She could be absolutely anywhere by now. That means she has to make the first move."

"What kind of a move?"

"I guess it'll be an exchange. Your dad turns over the evidence and Ellen turns over the kids. We promise never to tell on her or . . ." I paused, thinking. It wouldn't work. Ellen would have no guarantees that Barker had turned over all his evidence, because she didn't know what the evidence was. And how could she guarantee we wouldn't tell once our kids were safe?

"Or what?"

"Nothing. I'm just tired. So, you're sure your dad will come up here?"

"They're his grandchildren, Ben."

"What about us?" I stared at her, looking for a reaction.

"I'm more worried about the kids."

"Karen, I killed two people and put my own kids in mortal danger. You begged me not to, and I did it anyway."

"You've had to be strong, Ben. It's influenced you. I've been so dependent on you for everything."

"Is that why you married a bull in a china shop?"

"Maybe. I've loved you for your strength and your humor and your wisdom . . ."

"But now you've got Jesus."

"Yes. Does that bother you?"

"I don't know. You're not what I expected. I guess I was afraid you'd turn weird and I'd lose you."

"It's not like that. I love you even more now."

"What if something happens to the kids?"

She got up and walked to the window, pulling the blind aside. Dusk was creeping in, making the snow look blue. "You wanted the best for us, Ben. Our lives were in danger. All you could do was call it the way you saw it. If anything happens, I can only hope we'll be able to face it together."

"Stop white-washing it." My voice was harsher than I'd intended.

"Ben. Listen." She turned and buried her head in my shoulder. "It wasn't your fault." Her voice was muffled, and I felt dampness coming through my shirt.

"Yeah, sure," I said, my vocal cords going husky. "Just give me time. I'll get over it."

She broke away and stared at me. "I've never seen you like this. What's happened to you?"

"I killed two people, including one who trusted me."

"You're not superhuman. When are you going to see that sometimes you're bound to have flaws, make mistakes, be weak?"

"I'm weak now," I told her. "Does that make you happy? To see Ben Sylvester bashed to his knees?"

"No, Ben." There were tears in her eyes. "I'm just sorry you have no one to put your feelings of guilt on."

I mulled that one over. It was true — my anger at myself was tainted with loneliness. We're islands, and when the tragedy is our own fault there's a thousand miles of cold ocean between ourselves and the next person. There's a million miles between ourselves and whatever version of God we believe in.

"So what's the answer?" I asked.

"You're not ready to hear it."

"I might be."

"Tell me when you are," she said.

She lay down on the bed and closed her eyes. I went back to watching the snow outside. Though neither of us spoke, I could feel her support of me across the room, and it was good, like a warm campfire after a day trekking in the cold.

Time passed. The snow got deeper as darkness fell. Outside, they had switched on lights that accentuated the large white flakes as they came down.

"Ben?" Karen stirred and sat up on the edge of the bed.

"I'm here."

"No matter what happens, I'll stay with you." Her voice was steady, as if she'd worked it through and made up her mind.

"No matter what happens," I repeated. I didn't deserve her.

As if on cue, the telephone rang, blasting away the mood. It was past six, and Jim Barker was about to hear some bad news.

EIGHTEEN

He looked ancient, bewildered, the skin on his face reamed with wrinkles, his eyes flitting everywhere, never focusing on me for more than a second at a time. Mrs. Barker appeared weary to the bone, as if she'd had to carry her husband up the pathway into the lobby. Maybe she had.

We met them in the lobby. Barker, of course, took the lead from the beginning, his voice raspy. "How could you let them take my grandchildren?" This was directed at me.

"I couldn't prevent it." Why was I defending myself to this man?

"Where can you find me a gun? We'll have to go after these people."

"Jim." Karen's mom stopped him. "Let the police do it. They're trained."

"I can do it. Nobody's ever blindsided me before that didn't pay for it."

Pathetic. After spending years hating this man, now I watched him struggling on the fringes of reality, an object of pity, the old drive still there but derailed.

Karen's mother took Barker aside, not far enough. I heard her tell him, "Just wait over there. I'll find out what's happening and I'll tell you."

"You promise?" he growled.

"Yes."

He moved to a sofa about twenty feet away.

"I'm sorry, Karen." Her mom struggled with emotion for a few seconds. "We've been up all night on the plane. Jim couldn't sleep. He kept telling me stories of the early days with the company."

"How bad is he, Mom?"

"Bad enough. By next year sometime, he'll have to go into a home." She turned and stared wordlessly at her husband, who was already asleep. After all the agony she'd been through in her married life, the end of it must have been just one more kick in the teeth. Wherever the God of justice was, he didn't seem to be paying much attention to Mrs. Barker.

"Have they told you what's going on?" I broke in.

"Some of it. Our taxi driver was actually a policeman, and he gave us the bare details. But I can scarcely believe that it was Phil behind all this. And Ellen. Jim suspected them and gathered evidence. But I never believed that Ellen . . ."

Gently we explained the rest to her. She looked shocked, though I suspected she had ample inner strength to fight her way through just about anything. As far as I was concerned, Jim Barker had become a nonentity. All that was important was the evidence he held. I trusted that Karen's mom knew her husband well enough to convince him to release it.

"So it's Jim's evidence in return for the children," she said.

"Probably," I said. "It's been almost twenty-four hours and Ellen hasn't called yet."

"You don't think they'd —"

"No, Mom," Karen broke in. "They need the evidence. We'll trade for it and the boys will be safe."

She couldn't know how much my heart started hammering when I heard her talking like that. It wouldn't be that easy. If Ellen had any sense, she'd scheme to get the evidence and keep at least one of the kids until she was clear out of the country. In fact, she'd be smarter to skip out before she got the evidence, because she'd never have any way of knowing whether or not Barker was holding something in reserve. Why they hadn't left the country at the first hint of danger was something I was still mulling over. They'd admitted that they hadn't finished gathering the information they were selling to the Arabs. But wisdom would convince most people to cut their losses and get out.

Of course, neither Ellen nor Phil had shown an excess of street smarts despite their elaborate schemes. Phil had been stupid to hire only three cohorts, and Ellen should never have tried to entice us into Electar.

We got the Barkers settled in a room down the hall from us and got back to our room just an hour before the phone rang.

"I want to talk to Karen."

"You talk to me or nobody," I said.

"I'm making this fast." Ellen sounded rattled, angry. "Go to the post office in Kelowna and get a letter out of general delivery. It's in your name. No police."

The receiver clicked dead. Ten seconds. It could probably be traced, but the cops wouldn't find Ellen on the other end when they got there. Ten seconds. The only lifeline to our kids had beamed in and beamed out. I assumed the police had taped it, but I still stared at the receiver, willing it to come alive again and tell me more.

"What, Ben? Where are they?"

I told Karen what I'd heard, and she shut

her eyes, her lips moving but no sound coming out.

"It's a start," I said. "We'll get the kids back." Lies and deception. But what else could I tell her?

There was a knock on the door and Blakeny came in. "We got it on tape. The call came from Maple Ridge. They've sent out a car, but I don't hold out much hope for finding anyone."

"Unmarked, of course," I said. He gave me an I-wasn't-born-yesterday look. Maple Ridge. The name was familiar.

"Town west of Mission," he said, and I remembered riding there with Dave and getting an earful about Christianity.

"I'll go to Kelowna and pick up the letter."

"Hold on, Mr. Sylvester." Blakeny sounded authoritative. "We need to go over security arrangements before you start driving off hither and yon."

He sat down and explained that several officers were posted around the entrances of the guest ranch. While Plan A would probably be an exchange of the evidence for the kids, Ellen and Hans's Plan B could as easily be a direct assault on us.

"So you can't just let me hop in the car and get the letter."

"We've got to weigh this carefully. If there really is a letter, these people may have someone follow you into Kelowna to make sure no police are in sight. Or they might have someone waiting at the post office. If they want revenge, there's an infinite number of spots along the road that would be dandy for an ambush."

"What you're saying is that I can't get the letter, but if you don't let me get it my kids are as good as dead."

"We could send in a double with his collar up and hat pulled low. In this weather, it would look natural."

"You're joking, right?"

"Okay." Blakeny walked to the door. "We'll compromise. You'll go, but we'll protect you."

"I hope you're good at it."

An hour later, a taxi pulled into the guest ranch. If anyone had been watching closely, he might have noticed that the driver had the same build and hair color as me. Inside we traded clothes — he took my car keys and I took the keys for the taxi, with a third guy acting as my fake fare. The former taxi driver, now driving my rental car, left first. I followed, driving the taxi, ten minutes later.

Just before I left, Karen took me aside. "I'll be praying, Ben. Just take it easy. God will get us through. Don't put it all on your-self." She gripped me in a fierce hug.

As we descended out of the mountains, I watched the snow get thinner until brown tufts of grass appeared through it, then rocks and earth. The snow, fickle as usual, had faded from the bottom of the valley, leaving the landscape barren, the way it usually was. As barren as I felt.

The letter, if it was there, would probably be instructions on the exchange. Then we'd have to talk Barker into releasing his evidence. We faced quite a challenge despite Karen's optimism.

What worried me even more was that I had no illusions that Ellen was stupid enough to make a direct exchange. It looked like a valid offer, but I was sure she was going to try to hedge her bets somehow so she could be sure that neither Barker nor Karen and I would ever send anyone after her. Why hadn't she simply split? Did she think she was going to get away with the espionage and not have to leave the country? Surely she had had enough time to finish turning over the stuff to the Arabs while she and Phil were holding Karen.

I remembered my passenger. He'd been sitting quietly, probably waiting for me to break the ice.

"You comfortable?"

"Fine," he said.

"Have they briefed you?"

"Yes."

"My name's Ben."

"I know. Mine's Jack. Jack Connor. Are you going to need any directions?"

"Eventually. Right now, I suppose you're looking for ambushers."

"I don't think there's much danger to you," he said. "These switches are very effective."

"Have you worked on a case like this before?"

"No. But we've got a very experienced team —"

"Let's get past that, Jack. What are the chances of getting the kids back in one piece?"

"I really can't speculate. We're following the right procedures. You need to believe the best."

"Uh-huh." The conversation ended abruptly, and we spent an uneasy three-quarters of an hour until the cop directed me to stop at a restaurant on the east side of Kelowna.

Outside was my rental car — there had been no ambush. We weren't there to do lunch. After a quick clothes change with my double, I took over driving the rental. The police figured there'd be little risk of a sharpshooter getting me in the city.

Ten minutes later I was at the post office, alone just as I'd demanded. Not to any great surprise, I found a letter waiting for me — plain white envelope, no return address, mailed from Mission. There was one sheet of paper inside, and I read it as soon as I got back to the car:

There is a trail at the north end of Golden Ears Park that leads up Gold Creek to the lower falls (not the west trail). I want Karen and Jim Barker to deliver the evidence to the viewpoint at the base of the falls. No one else. No cops.

The date was four days away, two o'clock in the afternoon. It didn't surprise me that the note wasn't signed.

I sat there in the car, staring at the letter, reading it again and again until it seemed like my eyes had absorbed the words off the page. Gradually it dawned on me that there were things to do, and I started the engine. As far as I could tell, there'd been no one I knew hanging around the post office. I wasn't followed.

The trip back was a mirror image of the one in — meet at the restaurant, change clothes, pick up a taxi (different company, same driver), then a straight run up above the snowline. All the while I was gearing up for the next stage — negotiating with Jim Barker.

First there was the job of convincing the police to give us a free hand. Barker was a paranoid guy at the best of times. With his own employees conspiring to sell his secrets, and with his grandkids on the line, any heavy-handed police presence was bound to be dynamite.

We all knew what was needed anyway. The only possible course of action was to string Ellen along and hope we could grab the kids if she blinked. That meant Barker had to cooperate. I told the police that we had no idea how much his Alzheimer's might be clouding his judgment.

"Let Karen and me work it out. We know what's needed. He'll maybe trust us. I doubt he'll trust you."

They agreed. Karen went in first to talk Barker into meeting with me privately. Judging from the length of their conversation, it was a hard sell. When she came out, she looked shaken.

"Well?"

"He's not like you've ever seen him, Ben. Go easy. Don't get angry."

"Talk to him like a child?"

"No. Like a man who's hurting and scared."

"Bedside manner."

"Yes." Her look told me she was trusting me to say the right things. Somehow she'd lost her common sense.

Even with Karen's warning, I had to make quite a transition when I walked into Jim Barker's room. He sat in an armchair pulled up beside a window that looked out on a side lawn, now thickly covered with slowly melting snow.

"Mr. Barker?"

"Nobody asked for you." His voice was a growl built on a lifetime of domination.

"We have to make sure your grandchildren are safe."

"I've got the evidence," he said. "Briefcase on the dresser."

"Could I have a look at it?"

"Why? It's all there. You've never trusted me, have you? Never liked me, either." After a line like that there was little to say. "They tried to get you on your last trip out of the country, you know. Taxi driver was supposed to knife you. Karen told Ellen where you'd gone. She set it all up. You must live a charmed life."

My eyes popped at that one. Could Ellen's tentacles actually reach across two continents? Could she or Phil have gotten people to take out the real taxi driver and put in a killer? But other things were more pressing for me.

"I'm sorry, Mr. Barker, but I have to look at the evidence. We have to use it to get the children back."

"Take it." He flung a hand in my direction, exasperation showing.

The case was full of papers, most creased and jumbled. There were photocopies of invoices, a bunch of loose pages that looked like a diary, some newspaper clippings.

"Can you walk me through this, Mr. Barker?" I asked. He didn't answer. "Mr. Barker?"

"You got what you wanted. Get out of here."

"Are you releasing this information to me?" He said nothing. When I repeated the question, he put his fingers in his ears.

Back in our room, Karen and I and one of the cops went through the evidence, despair growing with every page. Nothing made any sense at all. Maybe Barker had some idea what his rambling diary meant, and why he had copied certain items. Maybe he knew why newspaper clippings about boat launchings and local weddings were important. Clearly, if he knew about the plan to knife me in a South American country, he'd had some kind of phone tap operating. But, as far as we could tell, Jim Barker's paper evidence was absolutely worthless.

NINETEEN

Six-thirty in the morning. The logistics of this thing were rapidly becoming unmanageable, but for the moment I was running up a trail into the bush, trying to get as far as I could before the birds woke up.

Golden Ears Provincial Park was magnificent mountain-and-trees wilderness intersected by zillions of trails. Gold Creek, which led to the falls, had two trails along its shores, one on each side. The east one, called the Lower Falls Trail, meandered on the flat to the base of the waterfall. The west trail on the other side of the creek was more rugged, more cut off from the riverbed. It branched off for a view from the bottom of the falls, but its main purpose was to take the hiker into a really tough mountain climb in the snow, with a necessary camp-out at the top.

Behind me, back about a hundred yards, Dave Mancuso's running shoes were flapping against the hard ground. I'd phoned him because he needed to know how we planned to end this. Jeff's sacrifice demanded that he know. But Dave had no intention of taking information from a distance — Edith, his wife, didn't even try to stop him.

So we were running to get into position during the small window between darkness and morning. This was where it got complicated.

If we were going to follow Ellen's instructions, Karen and her dad were supposed to go up the Lower Falls Trail alone and meet Ellen and our kids on the viewpoint at the base of the falls. They'd make the exchange, and Karen would go back with the kids and Barker.

But the risks were astronomical. As long as Ellen didn't know how good or complete Barker's evidence was, Karen and her dad were still a risk to her. If Ellen got a look at how feeble the evidence was, she'd realize she'd kidnapped the kids for nothing. Who knew what she'd do then?

The area was well used by hikers, but not many this time of year. With Hans and his sidekick still loose and available, Ellen could well be plotting something more deadly than her letter indicated.

There was no way Dave and I could use the Lower Falls Trail. Police officers disguised as couples and single hikers would be around, but there was too much danger that I'd be recognized. Dave, for his part, wanted to stick with me.

So we'd decided to go up the west trail at dawn and find a hiding place before anyone else got there. Part of our goal was to see what happened instead of having others tell us later. But another purpose was based on my suspicious mind — it was awfully convenient that a trail on the other side of the creek ended up within shooting distance of the viewpoint Karen was headed for.

We'd argued with the police. They wanted us out of the area entirely. Tough words had led to compromise. Dave and I promised to get ourselves established in hiding places before dawn. I'd wear a wire, and since I knew all the people involved, I could signal the cops when I spotted anyone. We wouldn't be armed, and we were supposed to stay out of any action that went down.

"Wait for me," Dave called softly. I slowed as he pounded up beside me. "Give an old man a break, will you? How much farther?" For an "old man" he was doing pretty well.

"About half a mile. Look, Dave, you don't have to do this."

"Do what? I'm just jogging with a pal."

"We can ease up a bit," I said. "It's still pretty dark. Be prepared, though, because any second a cop is going to lunge out from behind a rock and escort us to our hiding place."

We continued, the thick cedars and accompanying scrub hemming us in. Maybe it was the strangeness of the setting, but my mind began to strobe through disturbing images, each step flashing me another scene — our empty house, Jeff's gun in my face, Hans and Phil leering at Karen drugged out of her mind, Jeff disappearing under flaming rubble. I had no time to react to each one before the next one flashed through my brain. And every one of them accused me — of neglect, of stupidity, of life-threatening bravado.

So what was my problem? Why did I keep dumping on myself? Jeff had made his choices and died by them. As for my kids, I wouldn't have been any good to them if Phil had gotten me executed. The fire was our best shot —

"Police."

Just as I'd predicted, a figure loomed out of the diminishing darkness. "Ben Sylvester and Dave Mancuso," I said, winded.

"The path leads down there. Follow me."

We followed. As we went, the sound of running water increased until it was a roar. The falls would have been spectacular given a little more light. Even at dawn, they were impressive. The river bed was rocky and wider than the actual flow of water. Enormous boulders were everywhere.

"Climb down behind those rocks to the right of you," the cop said. "Stay out of sight of the trail we just came down, and try not to show yourselves to anyone coming along the trail on the other side of the creek. The viewpoint is over there." He pointed across the creek to the northeast. About one or two hundred yards away was a wide platform with a wooden railing around it, at the bottom of the falls.

"Before you get in place," the cop went on, "I'll rig Mr. Sylvester with a wire. Then stay down and stay put. There's a lot riding on this."

"Don't I know it," I muttered. We rigged up the wire while the cop explained how it worked and the kind of range we could expect. I wasn't paying much attention, my mind on Karen getting ready to bring her ailing father to the rendezvous.

The waiting didn't help. We were securely surrounded on three sides by rocks eight feet high, but it was hour after hour of squinting at the waterfall, panicking every time the odd hiker walked onto the viewpoint platform. We talked to one another softly, not daring to risk even the squirrels knowing where we were.

I explained again what had happened to Jeff. Dave was clearly moved, but he didn't interrupt before I finished.

"What was with him?" I asked finally.

"He cared about other people. Is that so strange?"

"The guy he tried to save was the same guy who ordered him beaten half to death just the day before. No one can tell me that's normal."

"No it isn't. But Jeff was following someone who said, 'Forgive them,' after they'd nailed him to a cross."

"So we're talking about a saint here? Jeff was a martyr?"

"No, just a guy transformed by Jesus, a guy who couldn't watch even his worst enemy die without doing something about it."

"It's really because of Jesus?"

"I expect so."

That stumped me. Jeff had been a messy mix of all right guy and basketcase, not what I'd expect from a holy man. But I couldn't deny that he'd sacrificed himself for a criminal he should have hated. I would have danced on Phil's ashes.

Time continued to move slowly. Two or

three people came to the falls and pondered the meaning of life before heading back down the trail. Noon came, and we opened the subs and juice boxes the cops had left for us. At least it was cold enough that we didn't need to fear food poisoning. No rain, but the clouds were threatening again. At this low altitude, we'd have a few weeks to go before snow would be a threat.

The time was getting closer. Karen. The kids. Within a few hours, things would change, though I had no idea in what direction.

One-thirty. Ellen appeared suddenly, along with Hans's sidekick Harold. And my kids were with her. My kids. I fought the urge to rush to their rescue.

"If I had a gun . . ." I said.

"You don't. Hang on."

"Where did they come from?"

"I expect they camped out in the woods overnight. Otherwise the cops could have grabbed them along the trail."

We watched, the kids playing a few yards downstream, not near enough to the river to be in danger, too far to touch, the river loud enough to drown out any shout. I didn't dare risk it anyway — neither of us had seen Hans yet.

Now the minutes stretched into agonizing

intervals of anxiety. Karen would be there soon, but the waiting was torture. My children were across the river and my wife on the way, and Hans was not above killing people, especially after the things we had done to him. I took a quick look all around but saw no one except Ellen, Harold, and my boys.

Then they were there, Jim Barker hesitating in his walk, Karen slightly behind him as if ready to pick up the pieces if he fell. I remember it that way. Karen held the briefcase. The kids, of course, reacted with delight, running to her, hugging.

True to form, Ellen was already heading for the briefcase. But Barker was unpredictable, and the whole thing started to blow apart when he rushed her, screaming something. I couldn't hear it over the roar of the falls. They wrestled over the case until Harold came up and knocked Barker on his back. Karen moved up on Ellen, then stopped when Harold pulled a pistol.

"Do something, cops," I said into the wire, but nothing happened. Nothing. Ellen had the case, the kids were standing there stunned, Barker was down, not moving, right at the edge of the viewpoint, and Hans's pal had the gun.

"Move in," I pleaded. Nothing. Dave

grabbed my arm and shook his head as if to say, "Don't try anything stupid. It's too risky."

That was when I caught the motion out of the corner of my eye. To my left, soundless, slinking out of the brush onto the riverbed, was Hans, with a scoped rifle in his hand. He hadn't seen us yet. His objective was a boulder about thirty feet from us. We ducked back as he turned his head for a second.

By the time he reached the rock, we were out of our hiding place and moving down behind him. There was no way to signal the cops that would get them there before us. The sound of the falls masked the grating of our shoes on the river stones.

Hans had the gun up and ready before we got within fifteen feet of him over the treacherous terrain. We ran, risking all, lunging at him just as the rifle cracked. I grabbed Hans's collar and dragged him backwards. Off balance, he yelled and fell onto the rocks, clutching at the rifle.

Dave came up beside me and stomped on Hans's arm — two, three, four times — before he weakened enough to give up his weapon. Both of us tried to hold him down, but he struggled like a wild man, cursing, trying to bite us.

"Get a cop in here now!" I shouted into the wire. We were still invisible to the viewpoint because of the boulder Hans had been hiding behind, but I hoped the police on our side of the river could see us clearly. I wanted Hans out of the action. The thought of who or what he had shot before we reached him was driving me wild.

I couldn't hold him. Dave, across from me, was trying to pin his legs. From the redness in Dave's face, he was at the limits of his strength. "Come on!" I shouted, suspecting the wire was a dud.

Then, out of nowhere, two men emerged and took over. With a double snap of handcuffs, Hans was out of it and I could take a look across the creek. Karen and the kids were out of sight, Ellen and Hans's pal stood staring, and Jim Barker was still down, not moving at all.

Maybe there was hope. Had Karen somehow gotten the kids out of there, using the distraction from the rifle shot? But my elation lasted about five seconds. Harold still had the gun, and Karen was coming out from behind a large tree trunk. The boys were beside her.

She emerged slowly and then rushed across the few feet to her father. Barker was still down, and she pulled him up to cradle him on her knee. When she put one of her hands to her face, I knew where Hans had aimed his bullet.

Ellen grabbed Karen roughly and pulled her out from under Barker. There was a broad red streak down Karen's clothes. Harold motioned with the gun as the lot of them headed back down the Lower Falls Trail. All of them but Jim Barker.

TWENTY

"They're going back down the trail. Why isn't anyone doing anything?" It was clear that the two officers holding Hans didn't appreciate my involvement.

"We have people all over the area, Mr. Sylvester. They'll move in when it's clear. If they don't see an opening, one of our sharpshooters will try for a head shot on the man with the gun."

"Let the cops do it, Ben," Dave said, but I was already turning and running down the trail. There were shouts behind me, at least one guy running, but I knew I could outpace them.

A plan was formulating in my mind. It was risky and depended on too many uncontrollable factors, but I wasn't going to trust my family to the accuracy of a police rifleman.

I slowed a bit — no point in being totally thrashed too soon. It would take at least forty minutes for Ellen and Harold, along with Karen and the kids, to reach the parking lot. While there were few cops on my side of the river, there would be lots of them near the parking lot on the other side. I hoped I could figure out how to get past them.

As I jogged, conserving energy, the enormity of what I was planning began to settle into my consciousness. I was a trained negotiator about to deal with a couple of loose cannons who had very little to lose.

The trees sped by on either side, but I was in no mood to enjoy nature. "Suppose," some beast in me said, "Suppose that this is a remake of your stupid move with the fire in Electar. Suppose it's Karen or one of the kids that buys it this time."

But I sensed this situation would be different; it would be my life on the line. If only the police would keep back long enough to let this work itself out. All the while the voice in my head shouted, "Fool!"

One last steep slope down, a run along the road to the bridge, then I was at the parking lot for the lower trail. Two couples were hanging around, and the man belonging to one of them beckoned me over.

"Mr. Sylvester, stay out of this."

"I know what I'm doing. Where are they?"

"About three-quarters of a mile away."

"Are you going to try to keep me out of the action?"

"Yes." He reached for my arm, expecting

me to give up easily, but I shoved him and started to run up the trail, dreading this, wishing it was over. The cops hung back. What were they going to do — shoot me? I suspected that there were more of them in the woods off the trail, but by the time they got organized I was too close to Ellen and Karen for them to risk grabbing me.

I came around a corner and saw them up ahead, moving into a side trail that led toward the river. Not all of the trail was visible, but it seemed to curve in a loop, with the other end coming out just a few feet from where I was standing. I took it, hoping to head them off. My path opened up on a wide beach — sandy, some gravel, no trees.

And there they were — Karen and the kids in front, Ellen and Harold behind. Jack, my oldest, spotted me and ran forward shouting, "Daddy!" I caught him midway, marveling at the wave of emotion that hit me. Jimmie was close behind, and I hugged them together. If I'd been convinced they would have obeyed, I'd have sent them down the trail to safety. But I knew they wouldn't leave Karen and me.

Struggling to forget the gun in Harold's hand, I walked forward, holding one child's hand in each of mine.

"Ellen," I said, coming to a stop three feet

in front of her. "We're going to talk."

Panic flooded Karen's face. "What are you doing, Ben?"

"Shut up!" Ellen said, turning fiercely on Karen. She faced me. "You killed Phil."

"No, Jeff did that. Look, we've got more important things to deal with. If you want to make it out of here alive, you better listen."

A flame came into her eyes, and for a moment I saw the kind of person who could so easily terrorize women and children for fun and profit. A similar flame burned in me, but I beat it down. My own fury was irrelevant.

"What was your plan?" I asked her.

"Who cares at this point?"

"Because I have to explain your options to you. They're a whole lot fewer than you think."

"Do you really want Harold here to kill your family?" Ellen barked. "You must be crazy."

"Listen to me very carefully," I said, backing up a few steps and keeping my voice as even as I could. "These woods contain a couple of dozen cops. There's a sharpshooter with a sniper scope trained on that idiot's head." I pointed at Harold. He said nothing, but I sensed him shriveling.

Karen gasped audibly. For the first time I

noticed that her face was streaked muddy with tears. The kids were numb and silent, sensing big trouble but having no idea what to do.

None of that mattered — I was more concerned about Ellen's reaction. She could have gone berserk and ordered the sidekick to start shooting. Or she could have put her hands up and waited for the inevitable. Instead, she signaled Harold, who grabbed Karen and held her tightly against him. No sharpshooter in the world would have risked a shot at him.

"I don't believe you," Ellen said.

I called out, "Would one of you officers show himself?" A guy about thirty, dressed in bush coat and hiking boots, came out of the woods twenty feet from us. He had a pistol in his hand. "That's good enough," I said. "Disappear again." Obligingly, he faded back among the trees at the edge of the beach clearing.

"What do you want me to tell you?" Ellen asked, her voice flat.

"I couldn't care less right now whether you get away with your crimes," I said. "My only objective is to get my family away from you alive and well."

"Do we have time to negotiate?" she said, looking at the sky to the east.

"Sure. For starters, why didn't you leave the country when you lost Karen? Why snatch my kids and get Barker up here?"

"None of your business."

"This won't work if you won't cooperate, Ellen. I need to know your plans so that we can find a solution."

"I've got a solution. We'll take Karen, and your cops will give us free passage out of the country."

"You and this creep?" I asked, pointing at Harold. "In your dreams. These hostage schemes never work. You must know that."

"There aren't any other options."

"No? You must have something to bargain with. Maybe the names of your contacts."

"I've got something better. Your wife." Harold gripped her closer, making my blood boil. "Your kids too if I need them."

"You had to have some reason for hanging around this long," I told her. "The moment your pet monster Hans — he's under lock and key, by the way — the moment he blew it trying to kill Jeff and me, you must have known it was time to go touring in South America."

Ellen looked uncomfortable. "I get it," I went on. "You weren't done with the espionage. Either you had something more to sell or you hadn't gotten paid yet. Is that why you kidnapped Karen in the first place — to buy you a month with Barker off your back while you completed your filthy little deal?"

She said nothing, but her face told the story. Obviously Barker, even with Alzheimer's, was still enough of a danger that Phil and Ellen needed a hostage to keep him quiet. Karen and the kids were the obvious victims.

One more question. "Why did you want Barker dead?" I asked.

"Not my idea."

"Whose then? No, don't tell me. The people who were buying your secrets wanted him out of the way. What happened — did they refuse to pay you until you did Barker in? What would it matter anyway, with you out of the country, unless . . ." Unless there were other people in the company also selling secrets, people who needed protection from Barker's prying.

"This isn't getting us anywhere," Ellen said. "We're taking Karen. You get to arrange for the plane. Get moving. Now, Mister!" Somehow her words weren't spoken with the urgency I expected. Something was wrong. She looked up toward the east again. Buying time?

"Why did you give up trying to kill me?

You could have taken me out in Kelowna."

"I told you to get us a plane."

"Not until you answer my question."

"It's simple. We needed someone to convince Barker and the cops we meant business. If, that is, you were stupid enough to call the cops. Now arrange for that plane and safe passage to the nearest airport." Again a note of falsehood in her tone. What was it? Almost like panic. She kept looking to the east. What was going on?

"Get out of here!" Ellen just about lost it, her voice at full volume.

I decided. "No."

Ellen turned to Harold. "Shoot his wife. We'll take the kids."

"You do," I told Harold, "and the sharpshooter will remove your head."

"One of the kids, then," Ellen said, her voice dead. I couldn't believe she meant it.

"I don't do kids," Harold said.

"Then give me the gun."

Harold sneered. "The minute I let go of this, the cops'll be all over me."

"You're in a bind, Ellen," I said. "Give it up."

"I'm not as stupid as you think," she said, just as I heard the sound of a helicopter coming in fast from the northeast.

"You arranged for your own transport?"

She'd just been buying time, trying to get me out of the scene by telling me to arrange for a plane for her. I'd underestimated her, maybe fatally.

"Look, Ellen, leave Karen and the kids and take me. Your clown here won't do kids. Maybe he won't do women either. I'm a better hostage for you than Karen or my boys."

"Forget it!" Ellen shouted, her voice almost drowned out by the chopper, now a hundred feet overhead. "Kill him."

Harold, about twenty feet from me, fired just a second after I'd leaped sideways. I felt a tug on my left sleeve as I fell hard on the gravel and tried to scramble for cover. Goodness knows why — I wouldn't be able dodge a second one.

Then someone burst out of the bush and streaked across the beach, grabbing Harold's gun hand and flinging it up and outward so that the pistol flew in an arc and landed fifteen feet from him. I ran for it, shouting at the cops in the bushes to shoot down the chopper.

Whoever had jumped Harold finished him with a right cross as I took the gun in my hand. Karen was sitting on the ground near me, dazed.

"You okay, Ben?" It was Dave Mancuso

who'd taken out Harold. Dave. Pastor Dave. But I had no time for amazement. My hands were lifting, and the pistol was leveled at Ellen. Karen was safely out of the line of fire, and Dave was rounding up the kids.

But my hands were holding the gun, and Ellen was there, white, knowing that my movements meant danger to her, that my eyes were signaling a death sentence. I wasn't thinking about anything at all, totally blank, my hands and arms taking on their own existence, nothing in me wanting to hold back from shooting her.

"Ben! No!" Karen, her voice distant, approaching. She grabbed my arm but she couldn't move me. I was hardly conscious, my body living for itself, for its own craving. Then Karen was in front of me, running to Ellen, enemy Ellen who killed Jim Barker, draping herself in front of Ellen so that I couldn't get in a shot.

After that, police were everywhere, the chopper moving off, and it was over. Karen calling, "My dad?" as someone approached her, shaking his head. Karen clinging to me and crying, the kids hanging onto my legs while the cops led Ellen and the sidekick away.

Over.

TWENTY-ONE

Midnight. I sit staring at a test pattern on an educational channel while Karen and the kids sleep. We're home. Even our furniture is home, rescued out of a local storage warehouse.

The funeral for Jim Barker was four days ago, in Cleveland. It took some work to get clear of the Canadian police. They were polite, but they didn't appreciate my interference at Golden Ears Park, and they weren't too keen on the results of the fire in Electar or the details of my entry into Canada.

At the funeral, try as I might, I felt no sorrow for Barker, though I ached for Karen through the whole somber mess of burying the dead. She looked incredibly hopeless, as if she were saying good-bye to him forever. Maybe she was — how should I know? I've tried to get her to talk about it but she hasn't so far.

I don't understand all of this. You throw some religion in my face, and I'm supposed to grasp it, embrace it, even when it sounds like a retread from fairy tale time? Still, I

241

can't deny the change in Karen. And Dave risked his neck to save my life when I was seconds from taking a slug in the heart. Karen protected Ellen from me even though she knew Ellen had arranged to have her father shot.

Jeff. The police discovered only one body in the house — Phil's. No sign of Jeff, and they said the fire wasn't hot enough to obliterate his bones. Did he get out somehow? If so, why hasn't anyone found him? Maybe I killed a man who didn't deserve it, or maybe he's wandering somewhere, hurt or out of his mind. I was responsible for him, and I don't know where he is.

Enough.

Ellen decided to confess. Apparently her Middle Eastern contacts had played her and Phil like fish, refusing to pay the next installment until yet another piece of information had been passed on. When Barker caught on to them, they needed another month to wrap it up, so they snatched Karen and told Barker to keep his mouth shut. Then orders had come down that there would be no arrangements for a flight out of the country until the old man was dead.

I see now why they didn't want Karen to know they were enemies. If I was dead and Barker was dead, they might not even have to leave the country. Karen would own the company and Ellen would still be her friend. Trying to get Barker's evidence had been a good idea at first, but killing him was the only permanent solution.

It's strange sitting here in my own house, pretending that my family and I are just like any of our neighbors. But you can't remove an experience such as ours from your soul like some peel-off sticker.

What's the count — two (or three) dead, four traumatized, seven if you count Mrs. Barker, Dave, and Edith. People motivated by greed and uncontrolled by any sign of conscience have power to hurt and destroy. It's terrifying to reflect on how much damage they can do.

But I destroyed too, when I made a desperate bid for freedom in Electar. And I've been going over and over everything, sleeping badly, if at all, ever since.

Don't patronize me by justifying what I did. I've told myself all the reasons — they were going to kill us anyway; I had no idea Phil was hurt too bad to get out; Jeff went back in voluntarily; I tried to save both of them.

But it doesn't work anymore. I can't sleep because I'm afraid I'll see Jeff's face when I shut my eyes. I'm terrified to dream because

I'm sure the truth will rise up out of the dark place where I keep my secrets. And so I sit bug-eyed, watching a test pattern.

It's becoming clear that I can't hold it together.

Karen said, "Don't do it, Ben." She pleaded with me because she knew me, knew how far I'd go to win our freedom. I remember the look on her face, while I was thinking to myself: It's just Karen with another one of her endless fears. Didn't she realize I had to act, that Ben Sylvester would never just lie down and wait for a quick death?

So I went ahead and killed people. I thought I was doing the only thing I could, and I nearly killed my own children. I fought my enemies with all the energy I had, and now I can't figure out what's important anymore.

"It's okay, Ben," Karen told me tonight. "Life's going to be different now. Let's give ourselves time to recover."

And I saw it in her expression, that recognition that we'd entered a whole new game with new rules. She's got power. This religion of hers has given her strength, and my stupidity has left me defenseless, wanting to spend the rest of my life in dark rooms.

It all turned out great. My wild gamble at

the end paid off. So why do I start to tremble every time I remember Ellen telling Harold to shoot Karen or one of the kids? The whole thing could have ended in disaster. Hindsight tells me the odds were probably fifty-fifty. So Ben Sylvester risked them all because he could never sit back and trust the experts to do it right. He had to have it all in his hands — to live and die with one roll of the dice.

My father lived carelessly. We always knew when it was payday because he'd come home with a new treasure none of us needed, though it gave us pleasure. It was a wild ride, but never boring. Dad made sure of that.

"How will we eat?" my mother would say, her tone pathetic. But my father would laugh and take us somewhere fun because life's too short.

I remember that. "Life's too short," he'd say, his voice loud, his eyes glittering like a child's. He was in advertising, an ideas man, and somehow we did eat. But we treaded water in a sea of chaos, wondering where the current would take us next. I loved him fiercely because he refused to let anything stand between him and whatever he wanted to do.

When I was ten, my father died trying to

beat an oncoming train at a level crossing. I was angry, not so much at the fact that he died, but that he threw away his responsibility to make his family secure — he threw it away on a meaningless fling at trying to prove something to himself.

I saw his car afterward, mangled and foreign, the way my mother became the moment the policeman rang our doorbell. I was only ten, and suddenly I was father to her. She never recovered, was never much good for any decisive action from that moment on.

The ride was over. We couldn't live in the sea any longer, and I vowed, at ten, that I would never be like my father. For all the excitement of my brief experience with him, the man was a fraud, pretending to be a hero to me while all along he only wanted his own way.

I grew up fast while they all tried to run our lives — the welfare people, the schools, the police when I was caught stealing food at the supermarket. But I vowed I would take care of my mother. I vowed they would never make us their prisoners. We've talked about it, Karen and I. Karen understands what I fought for.

And now I find I'm a prisoner myself, Prisoner Ben, out to atone for the sins of my father, out to save the world, unable to do anything but leave a trail of wreckage behind me. I will not be like my father, but I find that I am my father's son after all. When Karen looked at me tonight, I knew that she knew.

Her look told me she thought there was a way out of the box I've put myself in. Her look said, "Ask me."

Maybe I will.

The employees of Thorndike Press hope you have enjoyed this Large Print book. All our Large Print titles are designed for easy reading, and all our books are made to last. Other Thorndike Press Large Print books are available at your library, through selected bookstores, or directly from us.

For information about titles, please call:

(800) 257-5157

To share your comments, please write:

Publisher
Thorndike Press
P.O. Box 159
Thorndike, Maine 04986